Cody st... Trudy Lynn's hand and blanched. "What if he'd turned it on you?"

"I never thought of that." Leaning slightly toward Cody, she dropped the crowbar. "Pretty dumb, huh?"

"Yeah." There was a catch in his voice. He didn't try to hide it.

When she started looking woozy, he reached for her.

Trudy Lynn stepped into his waiting embrace. "I won't be stupid like that again, I promise."

"Good. I don't think my heart can take much more excitement." He heard a stifled sob and began to soothe her the way he would a frightened child. "It's okay. I've got you. You're safe."

She leaned back slightly to look at him through teary eyes and said simply, "I know."

Books by Valerie Hansen

Love Inspired

*The Wedding Arbor #84
*The Troublesome Angel #103
*The Perfect Couple #119
*Second Chances #139
*Love One Another #154
*Blessings of the Heart #206
*Samantha's Gift #217
*Everlasting Love #270
The Hamilton Heir #368

*Serenity, Arkansas

Love Inspired Suspense

*Her Brother's Keeper #10
*The Danger Within #15
*Out of the Depths #35

VALERIE HANSEN

was thirty when she awoke to the presence of the Lord in her life and turned to Jesus. In the years that followed she worked with young children, both in church and secular environments. She also raised a family of her own and played foster mother to a wide assortment of furred and feathered critters.

Married to her high school sweetheart since age seventeen, she now lives in an old farmhouse she and her husband renovated with their own hands. She loves to hike the wooded hills behind the house and reflect on the marvelous turn her life has taken. Not only is she privileged to reside among the loving, accepting folks in the breathtakingly beautiful Ozark mountains of Arkansas, she also gets to share her personal faith by telling the stories of her heart for Steeple Hill's Love Inspired line.

Life doesn't get much better than that!

VALERIE HANSEN

Out of the
Depths

Steeple
Hill®

Published by Steeple Hill Books™

STEEPLE HILL BOOKS

Steeple
Hill®

ISBN-13: 978-0-373-87407-1
ISBN-10: 0-373-87407-3

OUT OF THE DEPTHS

www.SteepleHill.com

Printed in U.S.A.

Count it all joy when you fall into various trials, knowing that the testing of your faith produces patience.

—James 1:2–3

I never get tired of saying that Joe is the most important person in my life. He always will be.

PROLOGUE

"She's the last one."

"I told you she would be. She's real stubborn. We're gonna have more trouble with her than we did with the others."

"Nonsense. She's a woman. Alone."

"Not exactly. She's got a lot of friends." He winced at the string of curses that erupted from his surly companion. "Well, she does. And folks around here stick together. You oughta know that."

"I don't want to hear any more lame excuses. If you can't handle this job, I'll hire somebody who can."

"You threatening me?"

"I never threaten. I promise."

"Give me a few more weeks. I'll up the pressure. She'll cave. I know she will."

"She'd better. I'm sick of waiting."

"I don't know why you're in such a big hurry all of a sudden. It's gonna turn out just the way I said. It's a sweet setup. She doesn't suspect a thing."

"Yet."

"Hey, don't talk like that. She'll be ready to pack her bags and head for the hills before much longer. She's already jumpy as a cat."

"She should be," the man said with a self-satisfied snort. "She has plenty to be scared of."

"You said there'd be no rough stuff."

"That was before. Things are different now. I'm running out of patience. And time. I'll step in and clear up the problem myself, once and for all, if I have to."

"You wouldn't!"

"Try me."

"Whoa. Don't get all het up." He waved his hands in front of him, palms out, in a placating gesture. "You won't have to do a thing. Two or three more weeks and Trudy Lynn Brown will be finished. She'll be so down in the dumps she'll be beggin' for a chance to sell out."

"Selling's not enough. I want to see her business closed. Period. End of story."

"Yeah, that's what I meant."

"Good. You'd better make sure that's exactly what happens or she won't be the only one in deep trouble."

"I know, I know. But don't forget about those kids she's got workin' for her. If they get in my way it might slow down our plans a tad."

"Humph." He raised his boot and brought it down on a passing beetle. Its shell collapsed with a sickening, deadly crunch. "Anybody who causes too many problems for me gets the same treatment as that bug. Including you. Best you remember that when you're dealin' with the lady."

"Just promise me you won't hurt her."

"I'm through making promises, especially to you. Get her out of my way—or else."

ONE

"Good morning! What a beautiful day," Trudy Lynn said, stepping out onto the porch of her cabin to greet her elderly hired hand. "Don't you love the Ozarks this time of year?"

"Yes'm." Will took off his sweat-stained baseball cap and held it in front of him. "Morning, Miz Brown. Can't say it's too good, though. Maybe you'd best sit down."

She shaded her eyes and braced for the worst. "What now?" The look on Will's leathery face made her heart sink. "Not more of the same?"

"'Fraid so."

"Oh, no."

It wasn't fair. Not after all the sacrifices she'd made to keep this business going. She'd hung on and finally prospered when other campgrounds and canoe rentals around her had closed. This year, she'd even managed to buy a bit of new equipment.

"What did they do this time?" Trudy asked nervously.

"Took out three more of them new red canoes. Looks to me like we'd best put 'em in storage and use the old ones for now. You can't keep buyin' new ones if somebody's gonna go knockin' holes in 'em."

"I know."

Pensive, she stood at the porch railing and gazed fondly at the neat campsites arrayed beside the Spring River. Oaks and hickory had greened up, while dogwoods were almost done with their blooms. Every day, new varieties of wildflowers appeared, some with blossoms so tiny they could hardly be seen. The only thing spoiling the picture was the knowledge that someone despised her enough to try to ruin her.

"Okay," Trudy told Will. "Take Jimmy and have him help you load what's left of my best canoes on the spare trailer. I'll tow it down to Serenity and rent a storage spot to park it. I just hate to back down like this."

"What else can we do?"

"Nothing. We can't stay up every night to stand guard and still hope to function well during the day, especially not when peak season gets here. Besides, it's too dangerous for amateurs like us. And hiring a real security man would cost way too much."

"How 'bout that ornery little dog of yours? We could tie him down by the boats. He's sure to make a racket if anybody strange comes around."

Trudy Lynn laughed softly and shook her head. "You know Widget barks at everything, including rabbits and deer. He'd sound false alarms and keep us running all night long."

"Prob'ly." The stooped old man nodded sagely. "Okay, Miz Brown, I'll fetch Jimmy and we'll load up them new canoes for you. He's not gonna like doing it, though."

"What my cousin likes or doesn't like isn't your problem, Will. It's time he learned that his brains aren't the only reason I hired him. It shouldn't take all day to keep our accounts current. When he's not busy in the office I expect him to lend a hand outside, not sit around playing computer games."

"That, I gotta see."

"You will. I promise," Trudy Lynn said, smiling. "He's my kin. I can always threaten to tell Grandma Earlene if he doesn't behave. Otherwise, I'll fire him, just like I did that Randall boy."

The old man put his cap back on and hesitated, squinting against the bright sunlight. "You be careful who you rile up. So far, all we've lost is a few boats. I don't want to lose you, too." Smiling wryly he added, "I'd never find another job as easy as this one. Not at my age."

She chose to take him seriously in spite of his jesting tone. "You be careful, too, you old coot. I'd never find another helper as savvy and hardworking as you are." Will's throaty chuckle warmed her heart. "Now get going."

"Yes, ma'am. You gonna be tending the camp store?"

"No. The new girl's a fast learner. She can cope with the store. Farley's had enough training to handle canoe launches by himself till you're free. As soon as you and Jimmy get that trailer hitched and loaded, bring the truck up here, and I'll head for Serenity."

"Yes'm."

Watching Will shuffle away, Trudy Lynn marveled at his devotion. He was a jewel, all right, but he was no kid. How much longer could he keep working? Every spring she had to train a new batch of local teens because her prior employees had either grown up and moved away or sought better-paying, year-round jobs. Trying to operate both the campground and canoe rental without Will's steady support seemed like an impossible task.

She huffed in disgust. If the vandalism kept on as it had been—or escalated—she might not have to worry about doing without Will. There wouldn't be any business left to run.

Once in Serenity, Trudy Lynn decided to stop at Becky Malloy's to unwind before driving back to camp. She knocked on the screen door of the old stone house and was welcomed with a pleasant, "Come on in! I'm in the kitchen."

"It's just me." She pushed open the screen. "Mmm. Smells good in here. Has your aunt Effie been borrowing your fancy oven to bake again?"

Becky stuck her head around the corner from the kitchen. "Hi there! Nope, I'm the one making the mess. I hope my cookies turn out as good as Effie's always do. I've got company coming tonight."

"In that case, I won't keep you," Trudy Lynn said. "I just stopped by for a little commiseration."

"I'm getting real good at that. Never dreamed how often I'd be called on to help people now that I'm a pastor's wife. I'm busier than when I was church secretary."

"How's Logan doing? As a preacher, I mean."

"As well as can be expected. There'll always be problems. All churches have them, even Serenity Chapel." She tittered. "Congregations would get along a lot better if they were made up of perfect saints. Unfortunately, there aren't any of those available."

"Amen. Which reminds me of why I stopped by," Trudy Lynn said. "We were vandalized again last night."

"No way!" Her friend's mouth fell open. "What happened?"

"Somebody knocked holes in more of my canoes. I just dropped off the rest of the new ones at the storage yard over on Highway 395."

"That's unbelievable. What did the sheriff say this time?"

"I haven't told him yet. Why hurry? He never finds any clues. I figured I'd stop by his office while I'm in town and fill him in."

"Do you want me to ask Logan to look into it for you?" Becky asked.

"And distract him from his church work? Absolutely not. He's not a detective anymore. Besides, he never did have connections around here—and I doubt anybody back in Chicago has it in for me."

"You're probably right about that." A timer dinged and Becky went to the oven to remove a sheet of finished cookies and replace it with another that was ready to bake. "Well, if you change your mind, all you have to do is ask," she said, resetting the timer.

"I know. Thanks." Trudy Lynn eyed the tray. "I could

be talked into tasting a few of those if you have extra. I was so upset I forgot to eat breakfast."

"How about having a cup of tea with me, too? I need a break. I've been at this all morning."

"Sure." Trudy Lynn got two mugs from the cupboard and added tea bags while her friend put a kettle of water on to boil. "So, who are you expecting? Must be important to make you go to all this trouble. You *hate* cooking."

"I can do anything if I set my mind to it. Dad told me oatmeal raisin cookies are Cody's favorite so I made lots."

"Cody? Your brother's coming?" She felt the flush of her reddening cheeks. "I thought he was long gone."

"He was." Sighing, Becky joined her at the table. "He got hurt."

"Oh, no! When?" Trudy Lynn immediately reached for her friend's hand. "Why didn't you tell me?"

"I didn't even hear about it until yesterday. I guess Cody didn't want anybody to feel sorry for him. Dad didn't find out till Cody called and asked if he could spend a few weeks recuperating at his place."

"How badly was he hurt?"

"Bad enough. His leg was broken. But that's not the worst part. When he told his girlfriend he might always have a little trouble getting around, she ditched him."

"The one he told everybody he was going to marry? That's awful!"

"No kidding. Dad says he's really down in the dumps. That's why I invited him here. My father's at work all day and Cody has nothing to do at Dad's condo but brood about everything he's lost. I figure, if he's here with Logan and me, we can at least keep his mind occupied."

"What about physical therapy? Won't that help?"

"It probably would if he hadn't refused to keep doing it." Becky made a face. "He is one stubborn Viking."

"I'd never thought of him that way before. He does kind of look like paintings of Eric the Red. So do you." She blushed. "The reddish-blond hair part, I mean, not the Viking-raider-swinging-a-sword part."

"Glad we got that straightened out." Becky was chuckling. "Why don't you stop by for supper tonight? Dad will be here and I've already invited Carol Sue to keep him company. We could use a fourth. You liked Cody when you met him, didn't you?"

"Sure, but—"

"Then come. Will won't mind babysitting your camp for a few hours. I don't expect the party to last long. Dad wants to head back up north and Cody'll probably be worn-out, especially after the long drive."

"What if he's not up to being in a crowd?"

"Then I'll just wag my finger in his face and tell him to get over himself, like any spoiled baby sister would." Her smile grew. "I'll probably get away with it, too, since we don't have a lot of history together. At least I hope I will."

Trudy Lynn thought back to Becky's odd past, being kept away from her brother and father because of her mother's lies. She took a bite of warm cookie and chewed thoughtfully before answering, "I hope so, too."

* * *

By the time she'd finally made up her mind on what to wear that evening, Trudy Lynn was disgusted with herself for being so uneasy. She was only having supper at a friend's house, not going to a real party. It didn't make any difference what she wore as long as she was presentable.

She made a face as she pulled the camp pickup into Becky's driveway and parked. Apparently, her subconscious disagreed. She couldn't recall feeling this concerned about her appearance for ages. Not that she wasn't always dressed properly, especially on Sunday mornings. She just wasn't usually as aware of the details, like whether her long, brown hair lay perfectly in place or her nails were neatly filed.

The muted silk dress she'd chosen for that evening was a favorite, partly because it brought out the misty-green of her hazel eyes. An attempt at highlighting her lashes with mascara, however, had had disastrous results. The brush had slipped and her right eye was still smarting.

Peering at her reflection in the truck's rearview mirror, she ran one finger gently beneath her sore eye. At least it had quit watering so the remaining mascara was no longer making black smudges. She didn't want Becky's big brother to take one look at her and conclude she'd been the loser in a fistfight!

Thoughts of Cody Keringhoven made her pulse jump. He was handsome, in a rugged sort of way. And when he'd smiled at her and his blue eyes had sparkled so mischievously, she'd tingled all over, in spite of her vow to never get involved with another man.

Funny, Trudy mused, stepping down out of her pick-up and starting toward the house. She hadn't thought of Ned, her ex-fiancé, for ages. Perhaps she was finally getting over the disappointment of their breakup. It was high time.

Climbing the porch steps, she was about to knock when Logan pushed open the door and greeted her.

"Trudy Lynn! Glad you could make it. Becky told me she'd invited you."

"Am I early? I didn't see any other cars."

"No. Not at all." He ushered her inside. "Dan drove around back so Cody wouldn't have to wrestle with the front stairs while he's on crutches. Can I get you something to drink? We have iced tea, soda and lemonade."

"Nothing now, thanks. Where is everybody?"

"Becky's in the kitchen, chiseling supper out of the roaster, and Dan's showing Carol Sue the newest model of those fancy cars he sells. The last time I saw Cody he was parked on the couch in the living room. Why don't you go keep him company till everybody else gets back?"

"Maybe I should help your wife?"

"There is no help for her when it comes to cooking," Logan joked. "Besides, that's my job. I've gotten really good at salvaging burned food."

Trudy Lynn took a mock swing at him. "Cynic."

"Realist, you mean. Come on. I'll introduce you to Cody, just in case he doesn't remember meeting you before."

"Oh, that's flattering," she retorted, grinning. "I met

him at church, and again right here in this house last Christmas, besides your wedding. If he doesn't remember me after all that, I'll be really disappointed."

They entered the modest living room together. Cody was seated on the brocade sofa with one leg propped stiffly on the coffee table atop a throw pillow. Dejection had affected him so deeply he barely resembled the vital man he'd been. It broke her heart to see such a dramatic, negative change.

Logan made brief small talk, then excused himself.

"Nice to see you again," Trudy Lynn said, trying to sound upbeat.

Cody barely glanced at her. "You'll pardon me if I don't get up?"

"Sure. No problem. Mind if I sit here?"

He shrugged. "It's a free country."

Choosing to ignore his moodiness she perched at the opposite end of the sofa, taking care to avoid bumping the coffee table or his elevated leg. "I'm certainly glad it is. And I'm thankful for the folks who keep it that way, too. Were you in the army like Brother Logan?"

"No."

"Oh." Trudy Lynn tried a different subject. "Becky tells me you guide raft trips."

He glanced at his injured leg, then scowled at her. "I used to."

"You will again."

"Not according to the doctors."

Oh dear. No wonder he was bitter. Becky hadn't told her enough about his injury to keep her from saying the wrong thing and now she had her foot planted firmly in her mouth.

"Have you gotten a second opinion?" she asked, hoping to salvage something encouraging from their conversation.

"What for?"

Trudy Lynn couldn't help the tiny smile that threatened to spread as she said, "To see if the second doctor is as sure about your leg as the first one was? I think that's what second opinions are supposed to do."

"Very funny."

"I figured it was worth a try." Leaning closer, she lightly touched the back of his hand. "Look, Cody, I know you've had it rough lately. We all face problems we can't understand, especially when we're stuck in the middle of them. It's how we let those situations influence us and shape our future that matters."

He pulled his hand away. "You have no idea what I'm facing. Don't preach to me, lady. I get enough of that from my family."

"I see."

Trudy Lynn's initial urge was to apologize and commiserate with him. She quickly decided that would be the worst thing she could do. If he wasn't ready to look for the bright side of his troubles, then so be it. She didn't intend to sit there and argue with him.

Chin up, she got to her feet and smoothed her flowing skirt. "Okay. Have it your way. You can wallow in self-pity all you want. I'm going out to the kitchen to help your sister. It's her I feel sorry for. I can go home. She's going to be stuck here with you for who knows *how* long."

The last thing she saw as she whirled and flounced from the room was Cody's expression of utter astonishment.

As soon as he was alone, Cody sank back against the sofa cushions. That woman didn't understand. Nobody could. He was still struggling to accept what had happened—and he'd been there—so how could anyone else have a clue as to what he was going through?

That fateful day had seemed perfect for running the rapids. "This is it," he remembered shouting. "Paddles inside!"

The bow of the raft had cut through the high side of the channel and plunged straight into an eddy. Behind him, the Slighman brothers had been whooping it up like the seasoned veterans they were. It was the two younger men in the front of the raft who'd had Cody worried. The guy on the right looked strong enough to bench press a semi truck, but he was acting way too nervous.

"Okay. Brace yourselves," Cody ordered. "Here comes the *Widow-maker.*"

Busy keeping the raft away from submerged rocks, he only half saw his panicky client let go of the safety ropes, drop to the floor and curl into a fetal position.

"No! Get up! You're throwing our balance off!"

The pliable raft's pitch and yaw tossed the loose passenger around like a knot of dirty laundry in an overloaded washing machine. Cody strained to plot a safe course through the approaching cataracts. The trick was to be in the right place at the right time and let the river do the navigating. His biggest concern was how much deviation his passenger's erratic behavior had already caused.

"Sit on the floor and stay there," he roared. "Before you get us all killed."

Cody's muscles strained to master the treacherous river. His lungs labored, his body ached. Determination welded his cold, stiffening fingers to the oars. Squinting, he spotted a narrow, clear path ahead. *Thank You, God.*

Suddenly, the man he'd ordered to stay on the floor gave a strangled cry and thrust his head over the side. Cody had only two options: make a course correction and hope the water was high enough to skim submerged rocks, or press through narrows where the fool might be decapitated. He chose the rocks.

Blinding spray stung like tiny hailstones. Momentum lifted the raft high on the left side, depressing the right till it was pushed underwater, sick man and all. Helpless to do more, Cody watched his passenger wash over the side. Then, to his enormous relief, he noticed the man's hand was fisted around the safety rope.

"Feet first!" Cody shouted. "Lead with your legs."

Instead, the frightened man grabbed an oar shaft.

Cody passed his free oar to one of the experienced rafters behind him and dropped to his knees. "Let go before you wreck us!"

Instead, ice-cold fingers closed around his wrist. Already off balance, Cody was easily jerked out of the raft.

The frigid torrent closed around him, hammered against his chest, stole his breath. Muscles instantly cramped despite the protection of his wet suit. Something was wrong. Very wrong. Plunging into a glacial watercourse like the upper Tuolumne was always a severe shock, but he'd never experienced anything this excruciating.

Nearly out of his head from the knifing pain, he'd gritted his teeth and forced his eyes open. One of the Slighman brothers had taken over the oars and was steering toward shore. He'd thought then that everything would turn out all right.

How wrong he'd been. With every muscle nearly as knotted as it had been during the accident, Cody struggled to free his mind from the past. Perspiration dotted his forehead. He had the same intense reaction every time he was foolish enough to recall the events of that horrible day.

He had to get hold of himself before someone came back into the room and detected his temporary loss of self-control. Closing his eyes, he took a deep, settling breath and purposely visualized how he'd finally surrendered to his pain and had let the river carry him where it would.

Even now, he realized with chagrin, that terrible trip was far from over.

TWO

By the time Trudy Lynn reached the kitchen she was contrite enough to relate her whole conversation with Cody to her hosts. "And then I snapped at the poor guy and told him off. I always babble too much when I don't know what to say. I feel terrible."

"Don't," Becky said. "Sometimes the best way to show love is to disagree, especially when the other person is wrong. So, how did he take it?"

"I'm not sure. His mouth was still hanging open when I left him."

"Good."

"Good?"

Becky nodded sagely. "Sure. He's a lot more likely to listen to sensible advice coming from someone like you."

"He did say his family was getting on his nerves. I assumed he meant his father, but I suppose that could include you and Logan, too."

"Probably. Right now, everything bothers Cody more than it normally would. He's already gone through plenty."

"What, exactly, is wrong with his leg? He said he won't be able to go back to work. Is it that bad?"

"Could be. His knee was smashed. There's a lot of scarring and stiffness. According to Dad, he'd have to regain a wide range of motion in order to be qualified to guide the kind of trip he loves. Might eventually have to undergo more surgery, too."

"Oh, dear." Thoughtful, Trudy Lynn glanced in the direction of the living room. "Now I feel even worse about the way I talked to him."

Logan chimed in with a smile of encouragement. "Don't worry. From what I've seen so far, Cody can take criticism as well as he can dish it out."

"He certainly can dish it out." Trudy Lynn gave Becky a pat of commiseration. "Like I said, it's you I feel sorriest for. You'll be stuck here with him."

"Maybe. Logan had an idea. Until you told us how you stood up to my stubborn brother just now, I didn't think it would work."

Trudy Lynn took a step backward. "Whoa. I don't like the sound of that. What kind of an idea?"

"A brilliant one."

"That's what I'm afraid of." Looking from Becky to Logan and back, she was struck by how in tune they seemed. Thoughts, expressions and actions meshed as perfectly as if they'd been married for decades instead of mere months.

"Tell you what," Logan said with a smile, "I'll go keep Cody occupied while you ladies discuss how we can all work together to help him through this."

Watching him walk away, Trudy Lynn felt decidedly uneasy. Logan Malloy was not only her pastor, he was married to one of her dearest friends. It was going to be hard to deny either of them anything, even if she hated their idea. And they knew it.

Folding her arms across her chest, she raised an eyebrow at her hostess. "Okay. I can already hear the train whistles, so if you're going to try to railroad me into doing something, let's get it over with."

"It's just a thought," Becky insisted. "We don't expect you to commit yourself right away. All we ask is that you consider doing it."

"Consider doing what?"

"Hiring Cody."

Trudy Lynn's glance darted in the direction of the living room. She lowered her voice. "To do what? He can't even walk, can he?"

"Not without crutches. But we all know it's bad for him to sit around and dwell on his problems. If he doesn't get out and try to do something for himself soon, he may never regain his agility."

"Okay. Bring him down to the river to visit and I'll have Will entertain him with stories about the old days. That'll be plenty distracting."

"Thanks. I'm sure it will help. But I was thinking about a job."

"I *can't* hire him." Trudy Lynn was adamant. "I can barely afford the staff I have—and they're fully capable of doing any job I assign."

"I understand. It's all right."

"No, it isn't. Why don't you beg or plead or yell at me or something?"

"I told you there was no pressure," her friend said. "There isn't. Logan and I will be glad to take care of Cody for as long as he needs us."

"Even if he never walks on his own again?" It was almost a whisper.

"Yes," Becky said. "Even then. I may not have known him when we were children because of my kidnapping but he's still my brother. I'm not going to give up on him."

"Wow." Trudy Lynn gazed at her friend through misty eyes and gave her a brief hug before she spoke from the heart. "I wish I had a sister like you."

As soon as Becky had finished arranging a platter of roast beef and had filled serving bowls with the rest of the meal, she picked up the two largest dishes and gestured to Trudy with a nod of her head. "Grab those mashed potatoes and bring them along, will you? I'll come back for the gravy in a sec."

"No problem. This bowl isn't that heavy. I can carry the gravy boat, too."

"Okay. Just be careful, it's…"

Trudy Lynn didn't hear the rest of Becky's comment because her voice had been muted when she'd passed through the archway to the dining room. Oh, well. At least they were through talking about Cody's problems. That was a relief.

Following her hostess, Trudy was surprised and happy to note that the injured man was up and about. Logan hovered close behind him, obviously ready to assist if Cody had difficulty managing his crutches in the crowded room. Dan and Carol Sue another of the Malloy's friends from church, had already taken their seats on the opposite side of the beautifully set table and seemed engrossed in a private conversation.

Cody approached laboriously. Pausing to let him pass, Trudy Lynn smiled for his benefit. She knew she had to continue to treat him as if he were just like everyone else. The hardest part was subduing the tender feelings that welled up every time she looked into his eyes and read the depth of his suffering.

Still carrying the food she'd brought from the kitchen, she stepped back to give him extra room to pass. On the opposite side of the table, Becky gasped.

Scowling, Trudy Lynn gave her friend a questioning glance and mouthed, "What?" Was she still too close? She thought she'd allowed Cody adequate space to get by, even with his crutches, so why was Becky acting nervous?

Drawing back, Trudy felt her heel hit the base of the wall. The only way to get completely out of Cody's path now would be to duck back into the kitchen. Regrettably, she'd sidled away from the doorway while trying to accommodate him. There was no easy exit.

She pressed her back against the wall as he started to pass and raised both arms, meaning only to carefully lift the potatoes and gravy out of harm's way.

Becky shouted, "Be careful!"

Startled, Cody faltered.

Trudy Lynn followed her friend's line of sight. If the

pitcher and saucer of the gravy server had been one unit, the way she'd assumed they were, she'd have had everything under control. Unfortunately, they were two separate pieces. And the gravy-filled section was starting to slide!

She had only an instant to make a correction. Cody was too close! She had to protect him, even if that meant absorbing the worst of the mishap herself.

Dropping her arm, she pushed the leading edge of the saucer forward and gave it a quick flip. That wasn't enough to right the shallow pitcher but it did alter its trajectory and keep its contents from showering the injured man.

Everyone was shouting. Trudy couldn't use both hands to halt the spill because she was still holding the bowl of mashed potatoes. Her only recourse was to press the small pitcher against her chest and wait for rescue. Thankfully, the discussion in the kitchen had delayed the meal long enough to cool and thicken the gravy.

Cody quickly tucked one crutch under his arm and reached for the potatoes. "Here. Give me that."

"Gladly."

"Are you all right?"

She answered without looking at him. Now that she had a free hand she was focused on wiping globs of gravy off her bodice and catching them without dripping on the carpet. The task was daunting as well as disgustingly messy. "I've been better," she said wryly. "How about you?"

"Never touched me. I hope that dress isn't a favorite."

"Actually, it was." His undertone of mirth caused her

to pause and look up. Amazingly, the corners of his mouth were starting to twitch into a smile. "I thought it matched my eyes."

"Only if they're part brown," Cody replied. He inclined his head to study her more closely. "They are kind of brown, with specks of green and maybe a little blue. The right one looks irritated. Did you burn it just now?"

Trudy Lynn made a face. Considering the state she was already in there was no use keeping up any pretense of poise or refinement. "No. The gravy wasn't that hot. If you must know, I jabbed myself in the eye with a mascara brush when I was getting ready to come over here."

"Are you always this accident-prone?"

"Not usually. I did want to be entertaining tonight, though. How am I doing?"

"Pretty good, actually."

The humor in Cody's voice reflected his smile and warmed her heart. "Glad to hear it." Her gaze briefly passed over the others and returned to him. "I'm sorry I made such a mess. If everyone will please excuse me, I think I'll go see if I can salvage my dignity— and my dress."

Her hostess had dashed to the kitchen for a handful of paper towels and was thrusting them at her. "Here. Blot."

Trudy Lynn shook her head. "It's too late for that. Just stand back so I can make a run for it before I start dripping on your floor."

"I'm not worried about the carpet," Becky said. "I'm worried about you. Want me to come help you get cleaned up?"

"No. Stay with your guests. And please don't wait dinner for me. The way my clothes feel right now I'll probably give up and go home anyway."

"And miss my sister's infamous cooking?" Cody asked, still smiling. "They tell me she's been working on this meal all day."

"I know. I can't apologize enough for being such a klutz." Starting to turn away she paused and stared directly at Cody. Careful to deliver her remarks with a straight face she added, "Even if my dress was okay I probably wouldn't stay to eat. I don't much care for roast beef and mashed potatoes without lots of gravy."

She could hear him chuckling softly as she hurried from the room. Good. At least *one* positive thing had come out of the worst social disaster of her life.

Reaching the guest bathroom on the ground floor, Trudy Lynn heard a ruckus behind her. Poor Becky. It sounded as if there was more trouble brewing.

She was turning the knob to open the closed bathroom door when Cody's strong, deep voice rose above the clamor.

"No!" he shouted. "Don't open that door!"

What a strange thing to shout, Trudy Lynn mused. She knew Cody couldn't be yelling at her. All the guests and their hosts were accounted for in the other room, so she certainly wouldn't be intruding on anyone. The sooner she got her dress rinsed out and could assess the damage, the happier she'd be.

An odd clumping sound echoed in the hallway.

Ignoring it, she stepped into the bathroom and shut the door. Her eyes widened. Her breath caught. She *wasn't* alone.

An animal as big and furry as a black bear was napping on the floor. Before she could decide what to do, the creature opened its warm brown eyes, saw her, yawned and began to pant.

"You're a *dog*?" Trudy whispered. Her voice rose as she realized she was right. "You're a dog. What a relief!"

The animal apparently took her words as an invitation. It leaped to its feet with a lot more agility than she'd imagined anything that size could possess and in one lumbering, tail-wagging stride was crowding against her, clearly begging for attention.

Deciding to assert authority before the situation got out of control, she said, "Good boy. Settle down," and tried to push the overly affectionate canine away.

Using her hands was a mistake. The dog took one whiff of the traces of gravy on her fingers and proceeded to lick them with a pink tongue as wide as her palm.

Trudy giggled. "Hey, that tickles."

To her delight, the dog cocked its head and looked up at her as if it were in on the joke. Its nostrils twitched, sniffing the air. "Oh, no. Not the dress," she said firmly. "If you want any more gravy you'll have to wait till I bring you some in a dish."

The impromptu training session was going quite well until Cody banged on the door.

"What?" Trudy Lynn called.

"Are you okay?"

"Of course."

"Stand back. I'm coming in."

The sound of his voice had already excited the dog so much it was spinning in circles. When he burst through the door, it raised on its hind legs and put its broad front feet on Trudy Lynn's shoulders, bringing their faces nose-to-nose.

She twisted away. "Phew! Dog breath. Down boy."

"Sailor. Stop that." Cody gave the dog's collar a tug. It landed on all four feet with a soft thump.

Once again, Trudy Lynn held out her hands to her new canine buddy and let him lick her fingers. "He wasn't hurting anything. We were getting along fine till you showed up and distracted him."

"Nonsense. Sailor only listens to me. I took him to obedience school, but he's been a lot harder to manage since I got hurt."

"I'm not surprised. You've probably been acting overly cautious and he's sensing an opening to become the alpha dog. He'll gladly be the boss if you let him."

"You're crazy. He knows I'm still in charge." Cody tried to grab the dog's collar again and was almost pulled off balance for his trouble. "Go on. Get out of here," he told her gruffly. "I can handle this."

"Oh really?" Forgetting her stained dress and disheveled appearance, Trudy Lynn faced him, hands fisted on her hips. "And who's going to handle you when you wind up in a heap on the floor or break your leg all over again? It won't be your dog's fault if that happens. It'll be yours."

Sailor had left his arguing companions and was cavorting around the cramped room like a hamster in an exercise wheel. A very large hamster. In a very small wheel.

"Sailor. Get over here," Cody demanded.

The dog looked at him as if to say, *You've got to be kidding. I'm having too much fun.*

Trudy Lynn stepped forward and calmly said, "Sailor?" She pointed to the floor at her feet. "Come here." As soon as he obeyed she added, "Good boy. Sit."

"Beginner's luck," Cody muttered.

"Maybe." She nodded toward the door. "You go first. I've decided to wash in the upstairs bathroom, instead."

"Good decision."

As soon as they were both safely in the hall and the dog was isolated in the bathroom again, Trudy apologized. "I didn't mean to usurp your authority. I just wanted to show you how being firm will work with a big lummox like that. He's a Newfoundland, isn't he? I love him. I saw one like that win Best-in-Show at Westminster a few years ago."

"Yes. I'd heard they were an easy breed to train. Too bad Sailor's not as intelligent as he's supposed to be."

"Oh, I don't know. He's smart enough to have you buffaloed."

"I told you. It's different since I've been on these stupid crutches."

"I imagine a lot of things are," Trudy Lynn said. "And since I know you don't want to hear my opinion about making adjustments to change, I'll save my breath."

"Thank you."

"You're welcome."

"Are you about ready to eat?"

She glanced at her dress and grimaced. "I refuse to come to the table looking like this. Folks in Serenity may be relaxed and casual, but this outfit is way over the top. Give your sister my regrets, will you?"

"Nope."

"What?"

"You heard me. I'm trying your training method. No."

"That's for dogs, not people."

"Whatever works. Becky can loan you some clean clothes if you want. She's already warned us we'll sit there and wait for you till we starve, if necessary."

"It would serve her right if I came to the table just like this," Trudy Lynn said with disgust.

"That's okay by me," Cody drawled, raising an eyebrow and looking her up and down before breaking out in a quirky smile. "I think you should consider changing, though. Sailor's losing his winter coat. I don't mind gravy stains, but that black dog hair all over your skirt is probably a bit much, even for laid-back folks like Becky and Logan."

In the end, Trudy Lynn gave in and accepted an oversize shirt and slacks from her friend's closet. Hurrying to the table, she was relieved to see that the others had already begun to fill their plates.

Becky quickly explained. "Dad has to get going soon, so we finally started without you. I'm sorry."

"Not a problem," Trudy Lynn replied, smiling across the table at the older man. "Why don't you stay over and leave in the morning when you're not so tired? I know it's a long drive." She shot a quick wink at the woman seated beside him. "Besides, I'm sure Carol Sue would like to get to know you better. She's a widow, you know."

"Can't. Cody's going to need the extra bed," Dan said pleasantly. "I suppose I could get a room at a motel."

"Absolutely not." Becky was adamant. "If you want to stay over we'll make a place for you here. Somehow."

"Or, I could put him up," Trudy Lynn offered. She took a spoonful of mashed potatoes, then set the bowl down. "I almost always have a few empty cabins, Dan. If you stayed overnight at my campground, maybe you could help us by listening for the vandal who's been wrecking my canoes."

The platter of meat came her way and she grasped it firmly. Fork raised to choose a slice, she suddenly froze in midmotion. Her gaze met Becky's, then darted to Cody and lingered.

He noticed immediately and scowled. "What?"

"Just thinking," Trudy Lynn said.

"About what? Have I missed something?"

"No. I was just wondering. I do have some available cabins, like I said, and I could use help. Would you be interested in spending some time at my campground?"

Cody cast a disgusted look at the crutches he'd propped against the wall. "Doing what?"

Her growing enthusiasm made Trudy Lynn grin in spite of his dour expression. This was the answer to everyone's prayers, including her own. "Watching. I can use an extra pair of eyes. That's all you'd have to do. In exchange, I'd give you free room and board."

"I can get the same deal right here," he argued.

"Okay. What about Sailor? I have a river and woods for him to explore that are far from dangerous traffic. And you'll get a rustic cabin he can't possibly hurt, even if he sheds a truckload of hair. It's perfect. How can you turn down an offer like thât? Your poor dog can't spend weeks shut up in a bathroom."

"I know." Cody was pensive. "What's the terrain like?"

"Flat, mostly. My basic operation is down by the Spring River on an old floodplain. You'll have to climb to get to the camp store, but if you need groceries or anything, I'll be glad to bring them to you."

"It might work." He looked to his sister. "I know you had your heart set on having me stay here. At least you did until you found out I was bringing my dog. Would you be too upset if Sailor and I spent a little time roughing it?"

"Well, I suppose it would be okay, if that's what you want. A city lot with no fence isn't a good place for a dog. I'd hate to have to chain him up to keep him safe."

Trudy could tell her friend was having a terrible time suppressing a satisfied grin. No wonder. Becky and Logan were getting everything they'd asked for, with one notable exception.

"There is a small catch," Trudy Lynn said seriously. "I can't pay you anything. I'm sorry."

"When I worked, it wasn't because I had to, it was because I loved my job," Cody replied. "I have some investments that provide income. If you have Internet access I can tap into once a week, I'll have everything I need."

"I do! My cousin Jim uses it all the time. He keeps the camp books for me." She smiled and arched an eyebrow. "I hate math. Give me a sunny afternoon, a picnic lunch, a cool river for swimming or canoeing and I'm as happy as can be."

It wasn't until Cody clenched his jaw and looked away that she realized how her innocent banter must have hurt him. Granted, her stretch of the Spring River wasn't a thrilling rapids but the comparison was there just the same. She'd have to remember to watch what she said, at least for a while. There was healing for Cody Keringhoven in the peaceful beauty of her campground. She could sense it. That was the most important thing.

And if he actually managed to help identify the vandal who'd been plaguing her lately? Trudy Lynn bowed her head and let her hair swing against her cheeks to hide her insightful smile. If that did happen, she might consider his success a very surprising answer to prayer, but she wasn't going to hold her breath waiting for it.

THREE

Getting Sailor into the back of her truck hadn't been nearly as difficult as Trudy Lynn had imagined it would be. Loading his master into the front seat, however, had turned out to be a real trial. Cody's behavior had been far too stoic to suit her. There was no way to tell if she'd accidentally caused him pain in spite of her monumental efforts to be careful, and that upset her greatly.

"You don't have to pretend you're invincible when you're around me," she told him after they were underway. "I'm not your sister or your father. If your leg hurts, I expect you to say so. I want to know what you're thinking."

"No, you don't. You may think you do, but you don't."

"Try me."

"Not in a million years, lady."

"I'm only trying to help. Why do you insist on being so difficult?"

"I'm not hard to get along with. All I want is to be left alone. I thought you'd figured that out. Isn't that why you offered me a free cabin? To get my sister off the hook and give me some privacy."

"That was part of the reason."

He huffed. "You don't think I bought that crazy story about vandalism, do you?"

"It's not a crazy story. It's true. I've had six new canoes ruined already." She absently kneaded the back of her neck as they drove farther from the heart of Serenity. "I get a headache every time I start to think about it."

"Headaches? Hah!"

The irony and contempt coloring his otherwise simple exclamation made Trudy Lynn stare. Cody was shaking his head and peering out the window as if he could see something terrible hidden in the darkness. Something invisible to her.

She was about to ask him if the bumpy road was bothering his leg when he shivered, then said quietly, "If you think a few wrecked canoes can give you a head-ache, you ought to try killing somebody, like I did, and see how much it hurts."

Trudy Lynn didn't know how to respond to his star-tling confession so she said nothing. Chances were, Cody was referring to an accidental death. She wasn't going to press him about it. Not yet. There would be plenty of time to assess the root cause of his depression after they became friends. And they would be friends, she decided. Even if she had to beat him over the head with tough love and kill him with kindness!

That thought made her want to smile. She would have surrendered to the urge if she hadn't been worried about giving Cody the wrong impression. The last thing the poor guy needed was to think she was laughing at his plight.

The most entertaining element of their situation was her own reactions to everything about him. It had been a long time since anyone had flustered her enough to bring out her klutzy side, nor had she been this personally interested in any man for ages. She wasn't a prude. She was simply fed up with exaggerated male egos, thanks mainly to her recent disappointment in the one person she'd thought she could trust to be faithful. Ned's disloyalty had taken her completely by surprise. Thus, she no longer trusted her instincts the way she used to.

Cody had been staring at her ever since he'd dropped his bombshell. "Well? Aren't you going to say anything?"

"About what?" Trudy Lynn huffed. "If you think I'm going to stick my nose into something that's none of my business, you have another think coming." One eyebrow arched and she gave him a cursory glance. "However, if you want to tell me what happened, I'll be happy to listen."

"Never mind."

"Okay." She shrugged and concentrated on the curving road ahead.

"You really aren't curious? I mean, suppose I'm dangerous?"

That brought a soft chuckle. "If I thought you were, I wouldn't be here with you."

Cody agreed. "If I had my choice, *I* wouldn't be here with me, either."

"That might be a little hard to accomplish."

"No lie." He was slowly shaking his head. "You know, as many times as I've gone over that day in my mind, I still haven't figured out what I could have done to avert the accident."

"Maybe it was meant to be." Trudy Lynn saw his fists clench, so she elaborated. "What I mean is, maybe there wasn't anything that could have been done, at least not on your part. Most disasters are the result of a combination of errors. You can't hold yourself totally responsible."

Cody snorted in disgust. "Maybe not, but the dead man's relatives sure blame me plenty."

"I'm sorry to hear that. Have they been giving you a lot of grief?"

"Not as much as they've said they're going to give me. I've been warned I'll be sued. And so will the tour company I used to work for."

"What did happen, exactly?"

He gave her a swift, telling glance. "I thought you weren't interested."

"Hey, I never said that. I just told you I wasn't going to pry. You're the one who kept talking about it."

"True. I suppose it wouldn't hurt to get your take on it. You are in sort of the same business."

Trudy Lynn listened patiently, stifling any urge to interrupt his story by asking for details. By the time he was through, she'd heard enough to clarify the main points and make sensible comments.

"Surely, your clients signed a waiver of responsibility. Even I require that, and my trips aren't nearly as hazardous as whitewater rafting."

"Of course they did. The victim signed one just like everybody else. Only he lied about his age. He was big enough to be every bit as old as he claimed."

"But he wasn't eighteen?"

"Bingo. Just seventeen."

"Do you have a lawyer?"

"If I need one. I'm still hoping his family will cool off and not file suit." He unconsciously rubbed the knotted muscles in his thigh as he spoke. "I did all I could. If my knee hadn't snapped when he flipped me onto those rocks, I might have been able to save him."

"You did your best, in spite of being hurt, right?"

"Of course."

"Well, then…" Trudy Lynn shrugged. "What more do you want from yourself?"

The look of disdain Cody shot at her was a clear rebuke. Trudy Lynn took her hands off the wheel long enough to hold them up in a gesture of surrender. "Okay, okay. No more unsolicited advice. But I'm right, and you know it."

"Do you *always* have to have the last word?"

She laughed softly. "I try to."

Fireflies were blinking a pale, luminescent green welcome when Trudy Lynn pulled through the double gates of her Spring River Campground. Thanks to the lateness of the hour and scarcity of overnight campers this early in the season, the place was unusually quiet.

The dirt drive meandered in a lazy, back-and-forth pattern toward the flats beside the river. "I'll put you in a cabin near the canoe storage to give you a better view of the area where we've had most of our trouble," she told Cody.

"You were serious?"

"Very. I really do need someone to watch for vandals." She smiled over at him. "And, yes, I actually do have that problem, in spite of your doubts."

"Okay by me. Sailor and I will be delighted to stand guard. Figuratively speaking, in my case."

"Don't sell yourself short," Trudy Lynn said.

Pulling up in front of a darkened cabin she killed the engine, set the parking brake and climbed out. Sailor had been patient till they'd stopped. Now, he was straining at the safety tether that held him in place in the truck bed.

"Just a minute, boy. Settle down," she said, pausing to give him a pat and ruffle his ears. "Daddy first. Then you."

She circled in time to meet Cody face-to-face as he braced himself on his crutches and slid off the seat. "I could have helped you do that," she said.

"I may be crippled but I'm not helpless," he replied stiffly.

"Good. Then I suppose you can get your own bags?" Her eyebrows arched.

"Gladly." Cody groped behind the front seat and pulled out both his canvas duffel-type bags, letting them drop to the ground at his feet.

Trudy Lynn reached for one of them. He stopped her with an outstretched hand. "I said, I can handle it."

"I know what you said. But this is my camp and you're my guest. I'm not pampering you. I'd offer to help carry anybody's bags, whether they were able to or not."

"That's nice. Tell you what. Why don't you let Sailor loose before he goes nuts? He gets really agitated if he thinks I'm going to wander off and leave him."

"I can see that." Trudy Lynn ordered the Newfoundland to sit before she unfastened the tether and lowered the tailgate. His exuberance in scrambling out almost bowled her over.

The dog had made two galloping circuits of the pickup and had come to a stop at Cody's feet before Trudy Lynn rejoined him. "Looks like he's happy now."

"It doesn't take much to please Sailor. Food, water and my company. They definitely are a family breed, just not suited to my sister's fancy new carpet and furniture."

"Well, we fixed that."

She was about to reach for his bags again when Cody waved her off. "Wait. Watch this." He pointed to the strap of the largest one. "Sailor. Bring it."

The enormous dog took the handle in his mouth gently, as if it were as fragile as a kitten, and, with his bushy tail waving, proudly bore it along while his master headed for the cabin.

"What about the other one?" Trudy Lynn asked.

"He'll go get that, too."

She hurried ahead to open the door and flip on the lights. Any worries she'd had that Sailor might get excited and knock his master down were dispelled when she noted how cautiously the lumbering dog proceeded.

When the first bag was safely delivered, Cody sent him back for the second.

"Wow. I'm impressed," Trudy Lynn said. "How did you teach him that?"

"I can't take credit. He was a natural. From the time he was a pup he carried things around. Loved my socks. I used to leave them on the floor just so he'd have something to pick up and bring to me."

"A furry valet?"

"Something like that. He added more to the mess than he cleaned up, but his heart was in the right place so I encouraged him." Cody's smile widened as Sailor returned with the second bag, mission accomplished, and placed it at his feet. "It would have been a lot nicer if he hadn't drooled, though."

"So what? You were going to wash the socks anyway."

"Right." He surveyed the one-room cabin approvingly. "Looks cozy. Any special instructions?"

"Not that I can think of. If I'd known anyone was going to be staying here I'd have made up the bed ahead of time." She was already moving across the room. "It'll only take me a second."

"Don't bother."

Trudy Lynn sent him a grin over her shoulder as she whipped the plaid bedspread aside, unfurled a clean sheet and bent to her task. "Why? Does your dog make beds, too?"

"Not yet, but I'm working on it."

"Should be an interesting trick. Especially if you can teach him to stop slobbering while he works."

Cody made a face. "Yeah. There is that problem."

"This cabin has its own private bathroom," Trudy Lynn explained while smoothing out the last wrinkle in the bedding. "Towels are in the cabinet over there. So are more clean sheets if you decide Sailor needs to practice his tucking skills."

"Thanks. I think I'll wait on that till we get home."

"In that case, I'll say good-night and leave you in peace."

She was almost to the door when Cody said, "Thank you."

There was so much true relief in his tone she turned and smiled. "You're quite welcome. Both of you. I'll get Sailor's food and dishes out of the back of the truck before I go. Sleep as late as you want in the morning. When you're up and about, I'll introduce you to my staff. There aren't many of us. Will and I stay overnight. The rest come to work when I need them."

Cody's eyebrow arched. "Will? Your boyfriend? Husband?"

"Will's old enough to be my grandpa," she said with a subdued chuckle. "There've been lots of times when I've wished we were kin. I guess *old friend* describes him best. He takes a real proprietary interest in this place. I don't know what I'd do without him."

"I hope he doesn't mind my staying here."

"Don't worry. First thing in the morning, I'll explain everything to him."

"While you're at it, would you mind explaining it to me, too? I'm still not sure how I wound up here."

"Providence," Trudy Lynn said with a wide, satisfied grin. "I needed more security and God sent you."

That brought a wry chuckle from her guest. "If I'm the best God can do, I think you'd better start questioning His wisdom. I have."

"What an awful thing to say."

"Maybe. But I meant every word."

She sobered, eyes wide, and nodded. "I know you did. That's what makes it a lot worse than it would be if you were joking."

Cody was so exhausted he didn't bother to unpack. He sent Sailor outside, briefly, then lay across the bed, fully clothed except for his shoes. The Newf made himself comfortable on the floor and quickly fell asleep.

Sailor snored, as usual, while Cody stared at the rustic pine ceiling and wondered why his dog had so much more peace than he did.

Because he doesn't think of the future, Cody decided. No worries meant no stress. Too bad he couldn't share the dog's easy ability to drop off to sleep anywhere, anytime.

Relating the details of the fatal accident to Trudy Lynn had brought the tragedy vividly to mind for the second time that night. Not that the young man's death was ever far from his thoughts. That moment would never leave him, never let him rest the way he once had.

Why kept nagging at him, refusing to be rationalized away. Too bad it wasn't a question that could be solved like a riddle that had an actual solution. There was no answer to his conundrum—at least not one that included the benevolent, loving God he'd sought and believed in as a lonely, motherless child.

In that respect, his sister, Becky, had more faith than he'd ever possessed. He wasn't about to pretend he still had a strong belief in the Lord, even if that meant he didn't fit her idea of the perfect brother. As far as Cody was concerned, God had deserted him. Twice. No, make that three times. First when his mother had been killed, second when he'd prayed for the safety of his clients on the raft while fighting for his own life, and third, when Stephanie had walked away from the love she'd once sworn would last forever.

He looked down at his injured knee. It was throbbing in time with his heartbeats. Must be time for another pain pill, which meant he'd also need a glass of water. Well, so what? Why baby himself? He was going to ache all night anyway, just as he always did. At least the cabin was small enough to hop to the sink without crutches.

He swung his feet over the side of the bed and spoke to Sailor so the dog wouldn't be startled, leap up and topple him. "That's it, old boy. Scoot over. I'll be right back." The thick, black tail thumped on the bare floor.

Cody pulled himself upright by grabbing the head-board and stood quietly for a second to make sure he had his balance. The brace on his knee would keep it from giving out on him but there was always the chance of a sharp pain causing him to falter. He switched on the bedside lamp and started across the room. Seconds later, he heard a throaty growl behind him.

Grabbing the edge of the sink for support he stared at Sailor. The usually amiable, laid-back dog was fully alert. Had the vandals returned? Now that he'd switched on the cabin light, they'd know someone was close by. Would that be enough to scare them away? Cody hoped so.

Leaning against the kitchenette counter, he listened. Other than Sailor's rumbling, silence reigned. Whippoor-wills had stopped calling to their mates, frogs had ceased their rhythmic chirping, and even the noisy cicadas were still.

He tensed. The first thing he needed to do was grab his crutches so he'd be more mobile. Second, he had to keep Sailor from going on the defensive and getting into trouble.

"Sailor, come," Cody whispered, giving a hand signal as well. Hackles up, the dog had risen and was facing the closed door, clearly standing guard.

"Sailor," he hissed, "get over here."

The protective canine reluctantly obeyed, edging closer until Cody was able to grab his collar.

The door creaked on rusty hinges. The first thing that poked through was the long barrel of a shotgun! Cody tightened his grip on Sailor, braced himself and waited.

A weathered old codger stepped into the room and took shaky aim. The man was clad only in boxer shorts and a sleeveless undershirt. At the ends of his spindly legs, his unlaced hiking boots looked as though they were at least as old as he was. Maybe older.

Before Cody could decide whether to yell at him, surrender, or burst out laughing, the old man commanded, "Freeze, mister. And call off your dog."

"I've been trying to," Cody said. "Don't shoot. We're unarmed." He raised his free hand. "You must be Will."

"What if I am?"

"Trudy Lynn, Ms. Brown, told me about you. She was planning to introduce us in the morning."

"Says who?"

"It's the truth. I'm Becky Malloy's brother, Cody Keringhoven."

"I s'pose you can prove it."

"I have my ID right here." Cody produced his wallet and held it out.

Will motioned with a jerk of his head. "Bring it over here. Real slow."

"That's about the only way I *can* move." He pointed to the crutches propped at the foot of the bed. "I'll do better if you'll hand me those first."

"You don't look crippled."

"Well, I sure feel it," Cody replied. "I just got up to take a pain pill. Mind if I do?"

"Guess not." He lowered the muzzle toward the floor so it wasn't pointing directly at Cody or the dog. "Miz Brown didn't say nothin' about puttin' nobody in this cabin." He scowled. "We hardly ever rent it, 'specially not this time of year."

"So she told me. I'm supposed to be watching out for vandals while I'm here. I guess you know all about that."

"Sure do. That's what I figured you was when I saw the light." Bushy gray eyebrows knit. "I tried sittin' by that there window all night. Couldn't keep my eyes open. That what you're plannin' to do?"

"Not tonight," Cody said, drawing water and downing his medication. "Dad and I just drove all the way from Chicago. I'm beat. Maybe tomorrow."

Thumbing the shotgun open to extract the shells, the old man nodded. "Suits me. Sorry if I scared ya. I'm goin' back to bed. You be all right?"

"Fine. Thanks. See you in the morning?"

"You betcha," Will said. "In case you're wonderin', I'm gonna go talk to Miz Brown before I turn in, see if your story checks."

"I wouldn't have it any other way," Cody said with a grin. "She's lucky to have you."

"Sure is." He eyed the now complacent-looking, panting dog. "Big fella, ain't he? What's his name?"

"Sailor."

Will chuckled. "Well, well. Me, too. Spent many a happy year as a merchant seaman before I finally decided to settle down. I take it he loves the water."

"I think he'd rather swim than eat," Cody said. "Newfoundlands are related to Labrador retrievers, just bigger and a lot more hairy."

"That's the truth. Sure glad he's yours to feed and not mine. What all does he eat?"

Cody immediately thought of Trudy Lynn's messy introduction to Sailor's fondness for beef gravy. Rather than mention it, he laughed then quipped, "Anything that doesn't eat him first."

"You'd best watch him around Miz Brown's little mutt, then. That Widget's got a nasty attitude."

"Uh-oh. She never mentioned having a dog."

"He's more like family to her. 'Specially since that fiancé of hers, Ned What's-his-name, took off." Will grimaced and blushed. "Forget I said anything about that, will you? Don't want her to think I'm carryin' tales."

"We won't mention it again," Cody vowed. "I had wondered why she was so fixated on this business. Guess she put all her energies into it after Ned left, huh?"

"Nope," Will said. "Always was nuts about canoes and camping. This place was perfect for her, right from the start. I think that's one of the things Ned didn't take to. Miss Trudy liked the outdoors a lot more'n he did." He lowered his voice to add, "You ask me, she loved the Ozarks every bit as much as she loved him, maybe more, and he knew it. Didn't surprise me when their wedding didn't pan out."

Cody nodded sagely. "Thanks for telling me. It'll keep me from putting my foot in my mouth." He managed another chuckle in spite of the growing discomfort radiating from his sore knee. "Good thing, too. These days, it's about all I can do to make my feet work together to hold me up. I can't afford to be chewing on one of them."

"And I'm standin' here keepin' you up and makin' it worse. Sorry, mister…what'd you say the name was?"

"Just call me Cody. Keringhoven's too hard to remember."

"Cody, it is. I'll look in on you in the mornin', 'fore I start my chores, case you need anything."

"Thanks. I'd appreciate that."

"Glad to do it. Any friend of Miz Brown's is a friend of mine."

Nodding, Cody bid him a polite good-night and waited till the door had closed before gritting his teeth. The pain tonight was worse than it had ever been, except perhaps for the hours immediately following the physical therapy sessions he had submitted to while hospitalized.

Seeming to sense his master's need for solace, Sailor licked his hand.

"Yeah, it hurts something awful," Cody admitted. "You know that, don't you?"

Sailor wagged his tail so vigorously his entire rear half swayed.

"Just be sure to keep it to yourself, okay? I don't want my sister and her church ladies fussing over me."

That much was true. Still, he'd agreed to come to Serenity for a recuperation period, knowing Becky would undoubtedly try to meddle and insist she was doing it for his own good.

"I must have been taking way too much pain medication when Dad recommended this trip," Cody muttered. "I can't believe I agreed."

In the back of his mind, however, another idea was jumping up and down and screeching like a squad of teenage cheerleaders at a pep rally. Could Trudy Lynn have been on the right track when she'd mentioned the possibility of divine intervention?

Cody immediately rejected that notion. If God had wanted to intercede on his behalf, He was too late. About two months too late.

He snorted derisively. Make that a whole *lifetime* too late. Considering all that had happened, there was no way he could ever go back to the unquestioning faith he'd leaned on as a lonely, confused child.

Of all the losses he'd experienced, that loss of faith left him feeling the emptiest.

FOUR

Trudy Lynn made sure she was the first person to knock on Cody's door the following morning. Her arrival was heralded by a chorus of deep woofing and a call of, "Hang on. I'm coming."

Fidgeting, she waited. When Cody opened the door she greeted him with a wide smile and a cheery, "Good morning." His clothes were wrinkled. His day's growth of beard was nearly invisible due to his light coloring but his tousled hair showed he hadn't expected such an early visit.

Nevertheless, he smiled. "I thought you said I could sleep in?"

"I know I did. I'm sorry. I just wanted to apologize for Will. His mistake was my fault. I should have stopped by his cabin last night and told him you were staying here."

"At least he didn't shoot me. Or my dog."

"Thank God—literally." She pointed to Sailor who was sitting behind Cody and panting so heartily he looked as if he was smiling. "Want me to walk him for you?"

"Not a good idea. He hates leashes. He'd probably wind up walking you. Besides, he's already been out once this morning. You're not the only one who's an early riser. My furry friend got me up at dawn."

"Did you rest okay? Is the bed soft enough?"

Cody nodded. "Actually, it's almost too soft. The less I accidentally move while I'm sleeping, the better."

"How about now? How are you feeling?"

"Fine."

Trudy Lynn could tell he was far from fine but she figured, if he wanted to deny his pain, that was okay with her. Dwelling on it was probably worse for him, anyway.

"Glad to hear it. Have you eaten?"

"No. To tell you the truth, I haven't even brushed my teeth yet." He rubbed his palm over his cheek. "Feels like I need a shave, too."

"And a change of clothes. Did you sleep in those? They look like it."

"Sure did. After your friend Will scared us silly, I didn't have enough energy left to get ready for bed." He glanced at his dog with affection. "Sailor was a great watchdog. Stood right in front of me and kept the dangerous old codger at bay."

"Poor Will," Trudy Lynn said. "He was really disappointed when he discovered you weren't the bad guys, come to ransack a cabin."

"I hope he put on more clothes before he went to your place to tell you about it. When he showed up here he was dressed in boxers and hiking boots. If he hadn't been pointing a gun at me I'd have laughed out loud. He has the skinniest, ugliest legs I've ever seen, except maybe on a scrawny chicken."

"That's because you haven't seen mine." Trudy Lynn was instantly sorry she'd been so glib. Cody was now looking her up and down as if he'd just discovered she was a woman, and she didn't like the awareness his assessing blue eyes revealed.

"You look nice in those jeans," he finally said.

Flustered, she averted her gaze and unnecessarily smoothed the denim. "Thanks. Now, about breakfast. How soon do you think you can be ready?"

"Ready? Ready for what?"

"The best biscuits and gravy in Fulton County."

"Are you asking me to go out to breakfast?"

"No." Her brow wrinkled. "I'm cooking. Actually, it's all made. I took the biscuits out of the oven before I came down here." She brightened. "Oh, I get it. You're thinking of your sister's cooking. Don't worry. Mine has won prizes at the county fair."

"That's a relief. But really, you don't have to coddle me. I'm perfectly capable of taking care of myself."

"I know that." She rolled her eyes. "Look, Cody. You might as well get used to folks being nice to you for no particular reason. Around here, people are friendly, period. It's not because you have a problem or because we feel sorry for you. Okay?"

"Okay." He shrugged. "I am a little hungry. How far is it to your place? Up the hill, right?"

"Right. But don't try to walk it." Trudy Lynn pointed to a squat, green, four-wheel-drive vehicle parked in the drive. "I'll do a few chores, then bring the ATV back and pick you up. How much time will you need to get ready?"

"Ready to ride that? About six months should do it."

"Cynic. I'll do the driving. All you'll have to do is shut up and hang on."

His wry expression when he said, "That's what I was afraid of," was so funny she couldn't help laughing.

Cody managed to shower and shave in short order. He didn't think it would hurt to humor Trudy Lynn just this once. Besides, he wanted a chance to ask her more about the vandalism before he got Will's opinion. He knew there wasn't a whole lot he could do to apprehend whoever had been damaging the canoes but there was no reason he couldn't at least try to get a description of them for the police. To his surprise, he was looking forward to having something constructive to occupy his mind for a change.

He was positive that he'd be able to mount the ATV successfully. How he'd stay on it once they were moving promised to be a bit trickier.

Trudy Lynn arrived in a cloud of dust and slid to a stop right in front of him. "Hop on."

"What about my crutches?"

"We'll clip them across the rack with a bungee cord. Come on. Gravy's getting cold."

Cody got on easily by keeping his injured leg straight and swinging it around and over, brace and all. Once he was in position behind Trudy Lynn, however, he was faced with the decision of whether or not he should slip his arms around her waist. His balance was off due to the knee brace and he didn't want to wind up flat on his back in the dirt, yet he hardly knew the young woman.

"You'd better hang on to me," she said, solving his dilemma. "This road's kind of bumpy."

"You don't mind?"

"Not at all," Trudy Lynn said. "I trust you."

"Thanks."

Cody did as she'd instructed, keeping his touch as light and gentlemanly as he could. Only in an emergency would he tighten his hold, he promised himself. Grabbing her like that would be a last resort.

It was a narrow waist, he noted. Yet Trudy Lynn wasn't delicate or prissy the way Stephanie had been. She was a healthy, active woman who treated men as equals, neither elevating them to sainthood nor denigrating them for being male. Though her casual acceptance was going to take some getting used to, he found he liked it, liked keeping company with a woman who had no hidden agenda. Trudy Lynn wasn't the type who picked out an engagement ring and started making wedding plans by the second date.

Whoa! Where had that thought come from? He didn't intend to start dating anyone for a while, especially not his sister's best friend. He'd been cured of any tendencies toward romance when Steph had dumped him. Besides, according to Will, Trudy Lynn was sort of in the same boat. Maybe that was why being with her seemed so pleasant. It was a welcome change to relax and not have to worry about whether or not he should consider a lasting relationship—or try to keep one from developing.

She broke into his thoughts with a question. "How're you doing? Am I going too fast?"

"I'm fine." Out of the corner of his eye he saw a dark blur. "Uh-oh. I must not have shut the cabin door tight. We have company. Sailor came along."

"That's okay," Trudy Lynn said, raising her voice to be heard over the roar of the ATV's motor. "He's a sweetheart. I'm sure he won't be any trouble. He might pick up a few bugs if he wanders into the woods but you can always wet him down him with flea and tick repellant if you have to."

"Does the stuff come in fifty-five gallon drums?" Her light laughter drifted back to him on the wind, lifting his spirits further.

"It must. They dip sheep, don't they?"

"Guess so. Since I won't be able to wrestle him into accepting the treatment, I'll have to leave it to you."

"In that case, we'll get him a flea collar instead. We can always fasten two together, end to end, if we can't find one big enough to go all the way around his neck."

"Clever. Are you always this smart?"

"Sure am."

She stopped the ATV beside a single-story offshoot tied to a larger, log building. "That's our store, camp office and laundry. I got tired of having to run over here to take care of late arrivals, so I built myself a connected apartment. Might as well live here. I'm on call night and day, anyway."

"It's very impressive," Cody said. "The whole campground is. No wonder you're proud of this place." The small yard bordering the private portion of the building was bursting with color. "I see you like to garden."

"Not if I have to fuss much. Those are all wildflowers that I've either transplanted from other parts of the property or started from seed. It seems like every day I notice something new starting to bloom." She shut off the engine. "Do you want to get off first or shall I?"

"Better hand me my crutches before I try anything fancy," Cody answered.

"Right." She giggled when Sailor galloped up and slurped the back of her hand. "I guess he remembers me."

Before Cody could answer, a yipping ball of brown-and-white fur raced around the corner. Teeth bared, it charged straight for the clueless Newfoundland.

Trudy Lynn screeched, "Widget! No!" and lunged, half on and half off the ATV, to intercept her little terrier. She'd have been successful, too, if Sailor hadn't practically bowled her over making his lumbering getaway.

Cody was hopping on his good leg so he could extend one of his crutches as a barrier between the dogs. When he saw Trudy Lynn losing her balance he redirected his efforts. Unfortunately, he bumped her with the tip of the crutch and removed any chance she might have had of righting herself.

She twisted in midair and landed on the back pockets of her jeans with an undignified, "Oof!"

Widget leaped into her lap, barking and growling while she clasped him tightly to her chest and told him, "Hush!"

Crutches set wide like outriggers, Cody half turned to check on Sailor. "You okay, boy?"

The big dog had laid its ears back, ducked behind him and was just sitting there, head down, quivering like a bowl of Jell-O in a California earthquake and staring up at his master with soulful brown eyes.

Cody glanced back at Trudy Lynn. She looked at him and grinned. Widget kept yipping. Sailor kept trembling. In moments, both humans had recognized the humor of their situation and burst into riotous laughter.

Trudy Lynn laughed so hard tears rolled down her cheeks. She'd almost regained her composure till Cody held out his hand and asked, "Want some help?"

That set her off again. When she quieted down enough to catch her breath, she answered, "No, thanks. I can manage. The first time you helped me was plenty."

"I didn't mean to bump you. I was trying to keep the dogs from fighting."

"I know. Poor Sailor. I don't think we need to worry about him attacking Widget, do you?"

"Probably not. I hope you can keep that ankle-biter from harassing my innocent dog. I came up here so he could enjoy a little freedom, not be traumatized by a psychotic terrier."

"Widget's a great watchdog," Trudy Lynn said, getting to her feet with the wiggly little dog tucked under one arm. She dusted off her jeans with her free hand. "Will told me I should tie him by the canoes at night and let him sound the alarm if we had prowlers."

"Did you?"

"No. Widget barks at everything, even fireflies. He'd keep me up all night, investigating nothing."

Cody followed her toward the apartment. There were already customers going in and out of the store. "Looks like business is good."

"It's picking up. This time of year is always kind of slow." She ushered him inside.

The place was small but cozy, with a definitely feminine decor, including lace curtains and floral-printed chair cushions. Through an open interior doorway he could glimpse activity going on in the store, proper.

"This is my kitchen. Guess you can tell."

"The stove and refrigerator were a dead giveaway," Cody teased. "Something smells great."

"Fresh biscuits. I told you I was a good cook." She pointed to another door. "My living quarters are through there. I wanted the kitchen out here so my staff could use it as a break room, too, if they wanted."

"You don't have problems keeping others out?"

"Not at all. The access is behind the counter so everybody can tell it's private space. I've never had campers wander in."

"Amazing. Aren't you worried about staying here alone at night? I mean, what kind of security does an arrangement like this give you?"

"All I've ever needed."

"Till now." Cody rounded the table and seated himself where he could keep an eye on the open door. "While we eat, I want you to tell me everything strange that's happened so far. Don't leave anything out, even if you think it's trivial."

"That might take a long time."

"Humph. Suits me. I seem to have a lot more leisure time than I need. If you've got the time to brief me, I have plenty of time to listen."

Trudy Lynn was carrying their dirty plates to the sink when she finished airing her concerns. "The only person I can think of who might have a grudge against me is a teenager I had to let go about a month ago. Name's Ronnie Randall. He was pretty upset. His father phoned me the next day and accused me of blaming the wrong person."

"What did the kid do?" Cody took a sip of his coffee.

"Petty theft. He helped himself to a case of sodas. I couldn't let it slide. It wouldn't have been fair to Ronnie, or to the others who work here."

"I totally agree. What makes you think he may be the one behind the damage to your property?"

"Mostly a gut feeling. Jim has seen him hanging around here more than once. Ronnie said he was just waiting for his girlfriend but I'm skeptical."

"Tell me more about Jim."

"There's not much to tell. He's a second cousin on my mama's side. A real math whiz. I hate book work. I'm lucky to have him."

"He uses a computer program, you say?"

"Yes. I used to write everything in a ledger. Boy, do I love letting Jim fiddle with the figures, instead. And is he fast! You should see him work."

"I probably will," Cody said, pushing away from the table and rising. "I'll want to borrow your Internet connection to do a little work of my own while I'm here. Remember?"

"Of course. I'll tell Jim to let you know when he's not going to be using the computer."

"That'll be fine. I'd also like a list of names and addresses for all your employees, even the seasonal ones, for the past two years. I don't want to overlook any angle." He noticed her quizzical expression. "What?"

"You're taking this a lot more seriously than I thought you would. What if there's no big, scary conspiracy? What if it's just a couple of kids who think it's fun to break things?"

"Then we'll catch them in the act, and they'll find out differently," he said.

"I don't want you to go to a lot of trouble. I mean, our deal was for you to watch from the cabin in exchange for rent. That's all I expect."

Thoughtful for long moments, Cody finally said, "Look. When I opened my eyes this morning it hit me. This is the first time since my accident that I've looked forward to getting out of bed and doing something. Anything. Being useful is a feeling I've missed and I don't want to lose it. Can you understand that?"

"Yes. Completely. I feel the same way about running this campground. Even bad days are better than my life was before I opened. And the good days are wonderful. The Lord's blessed me beyond my wildest dreams. That's one reason why I'll never sell or quit, no matter what."

"Quit? I thought you said business was good."

"It is. And believe me, I'm not complaining. I just

don't understand why all the other canoe rentals on this part of the river have closed in the past year or so."

Cody scowled. "*All* of them?"

"The closest ones," she said. "There were three others when I opened. I'm a little farther upriver but that shouldn't make any difference. If a client wants a longer ride, we just drive them to a distant point, launch from there and pick them up when they drift back down."

"Makes sense. We used to do the same thing on the Tuolumne. For Class I, II or III rapids we used a different stretch of the river."

"You ran Class IV and V, didn't you?"

"Usually." Cody glanced at his knee and gritted his teeth. "I really miss it."

"I'm sure you do."

He stared at her, waiting. "Well?"

"Well, what?"

"Aren't you going to tell me how lucky I am to be alive? Everybody else does."

"Hey, not me." Trudy Lynn held up both hands, palms out. "You warned me not to preach so I'm not preaching." She gave him a sweet, knowing smile. "But don't expect me, or Becky, or any of our friends to stop talking about God's influence in our lives. This part of the country isn't called the Bible Belt for nothing."

"Yeah. I didn't think of that when I decided to visit my sister." He turned and started away. "Thanks for breakfast. I'm going to go outside and check on Sailor. Hang on to your ankle-biter when I open the door, will you?"

"Sure. No problem. Come here, Widget. That's a good boy." She lifted her little dog in her arms. "Got him."

Though she'd sounded glib and unconcerned, Cody knew she was watching him laboriously making his way across the room and he wished mightily that he had his formerly steady gait. He'd always taken strength and agility for granted. Now that he was having to grit his teeth and work for every step, he realized just how much he'd lost.

It made him angry. Especially toward God. If there really was a God.

FIVE

Cody spent the better part of the day sitting on the porch of his cabin with his heel propped on the railing and Sailor dozing beside him. He'd read the information Trudy Lynn had provided. Everything seemed pretty straightforward. Her operation was small but well run and her seasonal staff members were teenagers drawn from the local community. Good kids. He'd made it a point to talk to as many of them as he could when they'd passed his cabin. One more was on duty in the camp store. He'd observed her working while he ate breakfast and couldn't imagine any threat originating with such a polite young lady. That only left getting to know Will and cousin Jim.

Cody smiled. The old man had failed to look in on him that morning as promised. Maybe Trudy Lynn had told him to stay away, or maybe he was embarrassed over their initial confrontation. Either way, talking to Will was going to be imperative. And the sooner the better.

He hailed a passing young man. "Hey there! You're Sam, aren't you? Have you seen Will lately?"

"Yes, sir. He's up by the office. You need him?"

"I'd like to talk to him," Cody said, "but not if he's busy."

"He always says he's busy, even if he's taking a nap." Sam sported a grin that accentuated the sunburn and freckles on his cheeks. "I'll tell him to come on down."

"Thanks. Make sure he knows there's no hurry."

"Yes, sir."

The warm sun and the ambience of the camp had been bathing Cody in Southern contentment all day. Compared to the cold wind off Lake Michigan at his dad's place or the icy waters of the Tuolumne, this was sure a pleasant place to lounge around. He sighed and closed his eyes. His knee wasn't throbbing ceaselessly, the way it had been. That, alone, was enough to make him glad he'd come.

"Afternoon," Will said, startling him back to alertness. "You wanna see me?"

The weathered old man was clutching his dingy baseball cap in his hands and looking as if he expected to be chastised. Cody smiled and gestured to the porch. "Yes, I do. Join me?"

"I guess I can spare a few minutes. What did you want to talk about?"

Cody waited until Will was seated in the other pressed-metal chair. "Trudy Lynn's prowler," Cody said. "Have you ever gotten a good look him?"

"Nope. Comes sneakin' around at night. I've seen shadows. That's about all."

"Where was he when you spotted him?"

"Down closer to the river." Will peered past Cody. "Don't think you can see that place from here."

"That's what I was afraid of. Okay. Tell me where you'd go if you were planning on sitting up all night."

"I ain't plannin' to."

"I am." He lowered his stiff leg and rubbed his thigh through the khaki fabric of his slacks.

"That's clear dumb if you ask me. Wanna borrow my twelve-gauge?"

Cody shook his head. "No. I don't intend to try to capture anybody. I just want to get a good look at them so I can give the sheriff a description."

The old man cackled. "Okay. It's your funeral."

"I certainly hope not," Cody gibed. "What makes you say that?"

"I'm not laughin' at you," Will said. "I'm laughin' because around here, our county sheriff is elected. Anybody can run. Most times, the fella what wins ain't much of a lawman. We figure we're lucky if he knows which end of a gun shoots and where to put the bullets."

"How about the man who's in office, now?"

"He's kin to just about everybody so I can't say." Will continued to laugh softly. "We only got two police cars for this whole county. Last I heard, one of 'em was broke down. That tell ya what ya need to know?"

"Pretty much," Cody answered, nodding thoughtfully. "Okay. Here's what we'll do. As soon as it starts to get dark, you come get me and help me find a place where I can hide and watch. Think you can do that?"

"Sure. But why ask me? Why not get Miss Trudy Lynn to help you? Be lots more fun."

Cody ignored the other man's knowing expression and conspiratorial wink. "Because I don't want her to know what I'm doing. You're not to tell her. Understand?"

"She'll throw a hissy fit when she finds out."

"Unless I spot a prowler, there's no need for her to know anything about it. Ever."

"There ain't much about the Spring River Miz Brown don't know. But I figure I owe you a favor after bustin' in on you last night, so I'll keep mum."

"Thanks. See you at dusk."

"Yeah. See ya." Will started away, then paused and turned back to Cody. "That fella Ned I told you about? The one Miz Brown was figuring on marryin' someday? He used to keep a lot of secrets. She didn't like it."

"This is for her own good," Cody replied.

"Don't matter. She still ain't gonna like it. Not one little bit."

Cody had let the old man help him to the river's edge and settle him comfortably behind a fallen tree. Moonlight reflecting off his metal crutches had made them too noticeable in the dark so he'd sent them back to the cabin with his cohort. There would be no need to walk until Will returned for him in the morning, anyway.

Smoke from a distant campfire layered across the lowlands, bringing back childhood memories of his father showing him how to cook hot dogs and roast marshmallows over an open fire. He smiled. Dad's love of the outdoors had certainly rubbed off on him, hadn't it?

Suddenly, a twig snapped. Cody slowly turned his head in the direction of the noise. Instead of the vandal he'd expected, he saw Trudy Lynn. Judging by her direct course she knew exactly where he was hidden.

Her "Hi, there," sounded far too cheerful for the circumstances.

"Get down before you blow my cover," Cody ordered. "What are you doing here?"

"Bringing you hot chocolate. I made a whole thermosful. I brought an extra cup, too. Mind if I join you?"

"Yes, I mind. How did you find out where I was?"

"Don't blame Will. I caught him putting your crutches back in the cabin. Even if he hadn't told me what was going on, I'd have found you sooner or later. Will said I was better off sitting with you than poking through the bushes alone in the dark. Don't you agree?"

"The only thing I agree about is how dangerous it is for you to be out here. Go home. Now."

"You don't have to yell."

"I'm not yelling. I'm stating a firm opinion. There's a difference."

"Not in my book there isn't." She plopped down on the ground beside him and ducked her head below the level of the fallen oak. "This is my campground. I pretty much go where I want and do as I please."

"Fine. Then catch your own vandal. I'm leaving."

"Oh, yeah? How? If I remember right, your crutches are back in your cabin."

"I'll crawl."

"Not on that sore knee, you won't," Trudy Lynn said.

Cody thought he saw a flash of sorrow in her eyes. When she immediately mellowed, he was certain of it.

"Look. I'll go back soon if that's what you want. Just have some hot chocolate with me first. Please?"

"If I do, you'll go home?"

"Yes."

"And stay there?"

"Cross my heart."

Sighing in resignation, Cody said, "Okay. Pour. But no funny business. One cup and you're on your way."

"Absolutely." She pulled a large thermos out of her pack and twisted off the lid. "I'll leave the rest of this with you so you can warm up through the night. It gets pretty cold out here sometimes, depending on the season, of course. I see Will talked you into wearing a jacket. That's good. I was afraid you'd be cold."

Cody scowled. "Don't you ever stop talking?"

"Not often."

"Then I know why you never spotted your prowler. He could hear you long before he got close enough to see you."

"Very funny." Trudy Lynn made a silly face.

"And very true." Cody waited till she'd poured herself a drink, then raised his cup to his lips. The liquid was scalding. "Ouch!"

"You don't have to chug it down and burn yourself just to get rid of me faster."

"I wasn't."

"Right."

"You calling me a liar?"

"Of course not. I just think you have a skewed view of life, of what's really important, that's all."

"For instance?" He took a more cautious sip.

Trudy Lynn blew on her hot chocolate and waited a few moments to answer. "Well, you might want to start by appreciating the good things. Didn't it occur to you that you were spared for a reason when you were pitched into that river?"

"I was lucky, that's all."

"Okay. Let's say you were lucky. Does that mean the man who drowned was unlucky?"

"I suppose so." He saw her start to smile. "What's so amusing now?"

"You are. Don't you see? If it's all a matter of luck, you just exonerated yourself. And if it isn't, if God is in charge of life and death, the way I happen to believe, you still can't take the blame."

Cody huffed. "Fine. Does that mean I should blame God for my limp?"

"If you want to. He can take criticism." She paused for another sip. "Later on, when enough time has passed that you can look at the whole situation objectively, maybe you'll see that what happened was for the best."

"I doubt it."

Trudy Lynn's smile was sweet and sympathetic when she said, "That's okay, too."

They sat in companionable silence till each had finished a second serving of cocoa. Stretching, Trudy Lynn zipped her empty cup back inside her pack.

"Well, guess I'd better keep my promise. You sure you'll be all right if I leave you here?"

"I have a bad knee, I'm not unconscious. Of course I'll be all right. Why wouldn't I be?"

She had to admit he had a valid point. "You win. I'm going. But don't blame me if you're freezing by morning and wishing you were back in your nice, cozy cabin."

"I promise to hold you blameless."

Clearly, he was teasing—and enjoying every word. Well, so what? If their back-and-forth banter amused him, she'd pretend he was winning their contest of wits. She knew she could give as good as she got. Truth to tell, she was enjoying Cody's wry sense of humor and the way his eyes twinkled when he was expecting a weird reaction to something he'd said or done.

If Cody wanted weird, she thought, he'd certainly come to the right person. More than one man had told her she was crazy, including her former fiancé. Thinking back on it, she was surprised to find the memory of Ned's censure no longer made her sad. Her spirit soared. What a wonderful, unexpected gift!

"You look awfully happy. What're you up to?" Cody asked.

"Just counting my blessings, like I told you to," she said. "I—"

A crash behind them made Trudy Lynn jump. Her eyes widened. "What was that?"

"I don't know. Hush." Cody pushed her head down. "Stay out of sight."

"Where did the sound come from?" she asked in a stage whisper.

"Down by the dock, I think."

Holding her breath and listening, she winced when a second blow echoed. The crunching, brittle sound was all too familiar. "That's one of my canoes!"

Cody hoisted himself up to peer over the top of the log. "Are you sure? I can't see anything."

"Positive. Fiberglass hulls always sound like that when they smash against a rock. Somebody's breaking up a canoe."

"Okay. Take a quick look. Can you make out who's there? Maybe give the cops an idea of what to look for?"

On her knees, Trudy Lynn eased higher so she could peer over the horizontal trunk. Rough bark flaked off on her palms. It was no use. Even with the help of moonlight it was too dark to see details that far away. "No."

She felt Cody's hand on her arm as he said, "Then get back down here before they spot you."

"If I can't see them, they can't see me," she argued. "We have to get closer."

"Absolutely not. We're staying right here."

"In a pig's eye." Without giving Cody a chance to talk her out of it, she vaulted over the fallen tree and started creeping, bent low, toward the sound of chaos.

"Wait!"

Trudy Lynn knew he was being sensible, but someone was tearing her life apart with every blow. She couldn't merely stand by and let them. No, sir. Not when she had a chance to intervene before too much more damage was done.

Near the rack of inverted canoes stood a bin filled with extra paddles. Trudy Lynn grabbed one in passing, hefted it like a batter stepping up to the plate, straightened and charged.

Cody heard her yell. His pulse had already been racing. When Trudy Lynn screeched as if she was either demented or under attack or both, he thought his heart would pound out of his chest. He'd never felt so helpless in his entire life.

Using his arm and chest muscles, he levered himself into a standing position. Deadwood littered the ground. Choosing a stout limb to use as a walking stick, he leaned on it and began to hobble toward the echoes of demolition and mayhem.

The energy Cody had to put into his efforts was tremendous. Sweat beaded on his forehead and trickled into his eyes, making them sting. Although the brace kept his knee from buckling, he still had to keep as much weight off it as possible, meaning his balance was poor.

He staggered. Tripped. Recovered. Pressed on. There she was! He could see her, silhouetted by moonlight. It looked as though she was alone. "Trudy!"

"Over here," she called back.

By the time Cody hobbled up to her she was sitting on the bare ground trying to catch her breath. "You okay?" he asked.

"Yeah. That was scary."

"Tell me about it."

She glanced up. "Hey! You walked."

"Correction. I hobbled." He gritted his teeth. "What the... What did you think you were doing?"

"Chasing off the bad guys." She rolled onto her knees and got up cautiously, wearily. "I could ask you the same thing. How come you followed me? Isn't that hard on you?"

"Not nearly as hard as sitting back there and listening to you scream," Cody said. He saw her start to sway and put out a steadying hand.

"I'm okay. Really," Trudy Lynn insisted. "The guy took off running the minute he saw me."

"What was he using on the canoes?"

"I don't know. I haven't had time to look." Taking a few steps closer to the dock she hesitated, then bent and picked up a metal object. "Probably this. I don't think it's one of Will's."

Cody stared, first at her, then at the crowbar in her hand. He blanched. "What if he'd turned it on you?"

"I never thought of that." Leaning slightly toward Cody, she dropped the crowbar. "Pretty dumb, huh?"

"Yeah." There was a catch in his voice that betrayed his emotional involvement. He didn't try to hide it. All he wanted to do at that moment was take this foolish, brave, outspoken woman in his arms and hold her tight, as much for his own consoling as for hers. Only his sense of propriety held him back.

When she put her hand to her forehead and began to

act woozy, however, he set aside his reservations, gave in to the urge and reached for her.

Trudy Lynn stepped into his waiting embrace as if she expected it. Needed it. She slipped her arms around his waist, laid her cheek on his chest and shivered. "I won't be stupid like that again, I promise."

His hold tightened briefly. "Good. I don't think my heart can take much more excitement."

"Mine, either."

He heard a stifled sob and began to soothe her the way he would a frightened child. "It's okay. Nothing bad happened. I've got you. You're safe."

She leaned back slightly to look at him through teary eyes and said simply, "I know."

SIX

The taller man clenched his fists and glared at his companion. "I don't believe it!"

"She surprised me, that's all."

"And you turned tail like a cur."

"What was I supposed to do? She came out of nowhere, yellin' and swingin' that paddle. She could have killed me."

"You had the crowbar, you idiot. Why didn't you stand your ground?"

"I told you. I wasn't expectin' anybody to get down there till I was long gone. She must have been waitin' for me. How do you suppose she knew I was comin'?"

"I've been wondering the same thing. Who did you tell?"

"Nobody. I never said a word about what we were up to."

"Not *we*. You," the first man said flatly. "I'm in the clear and I plan to keep it that way. Don't make me change my mind or get somebody else to take your place."

"I told you I'd handle Trudy Lynn, and I will."

"Like you did this time?" He spat into the dirt at their feet. "I should have known better than to include you in my plans. You're the one weak link."

"No, I'm not. I just had a little trouble, that's all. Next time, I'll finish the job, even if a whole posse comes chargin' after me."

His eyes narrowed menacingly. "Suppose you're arrested? What then?"

"They can't prove I was doing anything wrong."

"What if she chases you again? What will you do?"

"Do?"

"Yes, do. If she comes after you, I expect you to defend yourself. Understand? I want you to hit her. Hard. Got that?"

"But…what if I hurt her bad or…kill her?"

The taller man snorted cynically before he answered, "Then I'll go to her funeral and shed a few tears before I buy the place at auction and close it down." He smiled. "The more I think about it, the better that plan sounds."

"No way!"

"I was afraid you'd chicken out," he said with a thoughtful nod. "Okay. I'll give you one more week."

"Then what?"

Turning away he said, "You don't want to know."

The beam from a flashlight was bouncing down the hill, signaling the arrival of help from the main camp. Trudy Lynn stepped away from Cody, feeling like a teenager caught kissing her boyfriend good-night on her parents' front porch.

"I hope that's Will," Cody said. "I'm not looking forward to heading back to my cabin without my crutches."

"You did okay just now."

"Only because I was afraid for you," he said. "I imagine I'll pay for it later."

"I'm so sorry. I only brought you the hot chocolate to be neighborly."

"I know." He pointed to the place where she'd dropped the vandal's weapon. "Better not touch that again. We'll let the sheriff handle it. There may be fingerprints."

"Uh-oh. I never thought of that when I picked it up."

"That's because you're an upstanding citizen, not a crook." He cleared his throat noisily. "Speaking of your sterling reputation, I'm sorry about what just happened."

"What?"

"You know."

She certainly did. And a wonderful hug it was, too. Good thing it was dark enough that Cody couldn't see her face very well because there was an unusual warmth to her cheeks.

"Oh, that," she said, trying to sound nonchalant. "Don't worry. Around here, everybody hugs everybody. It's practically a given, especially among friends. No one thinks a thing about it."

"Really?"

"Really. You were just making sure I was okay, not making a pass at me, right?"

"Right."

"Well then, no problem."

Although Trudy Lynn was being totally honest with him, a hidden part of her heart wanted the circumstances to be otherwise. She'd thought she'd permanently cast aside all romantic notions long ago, yet Cody's nearness kept urging her to reconsider. Given his physical and emotional scarring, not to mention his hardheadedness, that was not a good idea. Not good at all. Then again, as long as she kept her wandering thoughts to herself and merely befriended him, what harm could it do? Even cynics like Cody needed faithful friends and compassionate comrades.

Speaking of which…a furry black blur the size of a pony galloped up and started to circle their legs with panting, drooling enthusiasm.

Will joined them a few seconds later. "Sorry 'bout the dog, Miz Brown. He must'a heard the ruckus and busted out of the cabin. I know I shut him in."

Cody sighed. "I don't doubt it. Sailor's strong enough to break the links in chains made to tether normal dogs. There isn't much that stops him when he makes up his mind to go somewhere."

Trudy Lynn patted the dog's broad head. "That's okay, Will. Mr. Keringhoven needs his crutches. Would you mind fetching them?"

"Glad to. You folks all right? I heard an awful commotion a few minutes ago."

"We're fine. Did you call the sheriff?"

"Yes, ma'am. Was that okay?"

"Perfect." She smiled at him. "We think we finally have a clue."

"Well, well. About time."

"That's for sure." Trudy Lynn noticed that Sailor had wandered away. She frowned at his master. "Where's your dog? He wouldn't have tried to track the vandal, would he?"

"I doubt it. He's no bloodhound." Cody cupped his hands around his mouth and broadcast a firm, "Sailor! Come."

Silence followed his call.

"Where could he be?"

"Best guess?" Cody sounded disgusted. "Swimming. It takes his coat forever to dry, too. That's why I keep him inside at night. The last thing I want sleeping in the cabin with me is a soggy dog."

"Can't argue with that. For your sake, I hope he's just sniffing a tree or something."

"Me, too. Sailor! Sailor, get over here." The words were barely out when Cody followed them with, "Here he comes."

Trudy Lynn looked around in time to see the Newf bound over an upside-down canoe and head straight for them. She didn't realize what he was going to do next until he stopped between her and Cody and started to shake himself. Repeatedly.

She gave a little screech and turned away in time to keep the flying drops off her face. The rest of her, however, was well showered. So was Cody.

"I told you," he said. "I should have known any dog with webbed feet would behave like a duck."

"No wonder he loves swimming."

"The mud he tracks in is the worst." Cody's eyes widened. "Oh, no."

"What's wrong?"

"The crowbar," he said, pointing. "Sailor's been stepping all over it. If there were any good fingerprints, after you handled it, they're smeared, now."

The sheriff arrived shortly, visited the scene of the crime with Will and took brief statements from Trudy Lynn and Cody before leaving. They remained seated on the porch of Cody's cabin, talking and unwinding, until long after the rest of the camp had quieted down.

"Later in the summer we'll need bug repellant to sit outside like this," she warned. "Mosquitoes can be deadly around here."

"They're deadly everywhere these days," he said. "Might as well be cautious."

"Right."

Cody was studying her profile in the reflected light from the cabin window. "What's wrong? You're awfully quiet."

"Maybe I ran out of things to say."

"That's never stopped you before."

She took a playful swing at him. "I'm not that bad."

"Could have fooled me." His smile faded. Now that they'd discussed recent events and he'd gone over her list of employees, there was a suggestion he wanted to make. He just wasn't sure how to broach the subject without putting her on the defensive.

"Listen, I know you like to handle things yourself,

and I commend you for it," he said, "but after what happened tonight, don't you think it's time to call in some professional help?"

"Like what?"

"Well, how about we start by asking Logan to do some background checks for us?"

"We? Us?" Her eyebrows arched.

"I just thought, since he's my brother-in-law, it would be best if I did the asking. You're welcome to approach him yourself if you'd prefer."

Trudy Lynn shook her head. "Becky already suggested it. The main reason I haven't is because I don't want to interfere with his pastoral duties. I can't believe how busy that poor man is, day and night."

"He won't be too busy to make a few inquiries for us, will he? After all, you do go to his church."

"I suppose it won't be so bad if we make sure he understands we don't expect him to drop everything and go back to being a private investigator."

"Then it's settled. We'll give him a call tomorrow and put him on the trail." Cody saw her make a comical face that was half frown, half smile. "What?"

She pointed to a sliver of sky visible through the oaks. "I think we'd better call Logan today. That sure looks like the glow before sunrise." She yawned. "No wonder I'm so tired."

"We've both been running on adrenaline. Now that its effect is wearing off, we're bound to feel exhausted."

"How's your knee?" Trudy Lynn asked.

"Not as bad as I'd thought it would be by now," he

confessed, eyeing his propped-up foot. "Ask me again in the morning."

"I just did. It *is* morning, remember?" Stifling another yawn, she stood and stretched. "Get some rest. As soon as I finish my chores I'll call Becky and see if she knows what Brother Logan has scheduled for today. If he's not too busy, I'll ask for his opinion. Okay?"

"Sounds good to me."

Cody purposely waited until she'd left before he tried to move. The calf muscles in his injured leg were tied in knots, but at least his knee wasn't throbbing. He used his hands to support and cautiously lower it. So far, so good. At least he hadn't had to stifle a shout of pain.

He pulled himself upright by tugging on the porch railing, then tucked a crutch under each arm before starting for the door.

Tail wagging, Sailor was already waiting there, ready to go in.

When Cody turned the knob, it came off in his hand! Disgusted, he looked at his dog. "So, that's how you got out. What'd you do, eat the inside handle?"

The Newfoundland wagged his tail and panted, his sad, brown eyes giving him a totally innocent expression.

Cody pushed open the door. Expecting the worst, he was relieved to note that the only thing Sailor had done to escape was chew at the knob and make a series of scratches below the lock.

Correction, Cody thought. *Not below the lock. Below where the lock would have been if the interior knob was still attached.*

He picked up the pieces and reassembled them as best he could, mostly to make sure Sailor hadn't ingested anything dangerous. When he was satisfied his dog had merely chewed the lock set apart and spit out the mechanism, he hobbled wearily to the bed, lay across it and closed his eyes.

In the morning, he'd use his cell phone to call the local hardware store and have them send out a replacement. That thought brought a quiet chuckle. Make that later *this* morning. Much later. Right now, he didn't care if the sun was rising or not. He had to get some sleep.

Although Trudy Lynn had made the initial request for Logan's professional advice, Cody had followed it up with a friendly call of his own, and the pastor had used that ready-made opportunity to pass along the results of his brief investigation.

Cody suggested Trudy Lynn drop by his cabin to discuss Logan's findings. She found him sitting on the porch in his favorite position, foot elevated, and paused at the base of the wooden steps. "Okay. I'm here. What was so bad that Logan couldn't tell *me* about it?"

"Like you said, he's a busy guy. We happened to be talking and he asked me to pass along some data, that's all. There's no conspiracy to leave you out of the loop, honest."

"I'll reserve judgment on that. Go ahead. What did Logan say?"

"Sure you don't want to sit down?"

"No thanks. I can't stay."

"Have it your way." Cody unfolded a slip of paper and began reading. "William Garfield Wilson, age sixty-seven, paroled after serving three years of an eight-year sentence in…"

"Whoa! You're telling me Will, *my* Will, has a prison record? Are you sure?"

Cody nodded. "The information came straight from the state police Web site. Logan was surprised, too."

She sank onto the porch step, shoulders slumping, and laced her fingers together around her bent knees. "What was Will arrested for?"

"Maiming a man in a brawl. It happened when he was in the Merchant Marines."

"That was ages ago."

"I know. There's more."

"I can hardly wait."

"Hey, I'm just the messenger. Don't grumble at me. I didn't make this stuff up."

"I know. Sorry. Go on."

"The other info you may already have heard through the local grapevine. Ronnie Randall? The kid you fired? His whole family has a reputation for being pretty unforgiving when they think they've been wronged. The boy's father and uncles have been arrested for getting belligerent numerous times. One of the kids working on the canoes told me they've been spreading the rumor you let poor Ronnie go because you're prejudiced against folks who have more influence than you do."

"Humph. That would be just about everybody in Fulton County, if it were true," Trudy Lynn said. "What I'm prejudiced against is thieves. I don't suppose anybody mentioned the little problem of missing sodas and candy from the camp store, did they?"

She was surprised to see Cody nod and refer to his notes again. "Matter of fact, they did. Ronnie swears he's innocent. Naturally, his family believes him."

"Naturally." She sighed. "Is that all?"

"Not quite."

The tone of Cody's voice caused her to glance up at him. "Uh-oh. What else?"

"Did you know that your cousin Jim is on probation? He was convicted of drug possession."

"Of course I knew. That was all a mistake. He was just holding a backpack for a friend. He had no idea there was anything illegal in it."

"That's the oldest excuse in the book, but okay. If you say so."

"I have to give him the benefit of the doubt. Jim can be kind of reckless when he's hanging around with the wrong crowd but he's not a criminal. If anything, he's a genius. I've never known anybody so gifted with a computer."

"Which reminds me," Cody said. "When did he say he could spare me an hour or so of time on the Internet?"

"I didn't get around to asking. Tomorrow's his day off. Anytime then should be fine. Let me know when you want to come over to the office and I'll send Will to get you on the ATV. Is that okay?"

"Sure. No problem. It'll give me a chance to ask him about his prison time."

"Don't you dare!"

"Why not? Aren't you interested in hearing his side of the story?"

"Not if it means making him think I don't trust him. People's feelings are more important to me than dredging up details of a past that can't possibly have any connection to my vandal."

"How do you know it can't?"

"I just do," Trudy Lynn insisted. "In all the years Will has worked for me, this is the first time I've had any problems. If he were involved, the trouble would have started long ago, and you know it."

"Probably. Unless whoever's been smashing your canoes was incarcerated till recently."

"A cell mate, you mean?"

"Maybe."

"I'd sooner believe fish could fly."

Cody chuckled. "As slippery as fish are, I imagine they'd have a real hard time roosting in trees. Birds wouldn't like the competition for food, either."

In spite of her worry over Will, Trudy Lynn couldn't help joining in. "Neither would the squirrels. Big catfish actually eat acorns if the nuts happen to drop into the water. I've seen them do it." She giggled. "You know, you have a very strange sense of humor."

"So I've been told. Doesn't it bother you that you always laugh at my crazy jokes?"

"Not at all," she said with a broadening grin. "After my trick with the gravy boat the other night, I figure my reputation has nowhere to go but *up*."

SEVEN

After thinking it over, Trudy Lynn decided that even if his closeness was a bit unsettling, Cody would be safer riding the ATV with her than with Will. The older man was cautious, sometimes to a fault, but his peripheral vision and reaction time left much to be desired.

She picked Cody up at 10:00 a.m. and drove straight to the camp office. Instead of making him climb the front steps and enter through the store, she ushered him through her kitchen and out into the central hallway.

"Like I said before, the computer is in that room over there. I've locked Widget in the bathroom so he won't bother you." At the arch of Cody's eyebrow she added, "It's a trick I learned from a guy with a *really* big dog."

"Glad to be of service."

"Speaking of service, Anne's on duty in the store. She's a sweetheart. I'll tell her you're working in here. If you get hungry or thirsty, just holler and she'll bring you whatever you want."

"I should be fine. All I want to do is access my accounts and see if I need to make any modifications. It won't take long."

"Investments like that have always scared me," Trudy Lynn admitted. "I prefer to put my money into things I can see and touch, like this place."

"I'm glad it's worked out for you."

"Me, too. It's been a long, hard road but I'm finally starting to see a small profit."

"Good. Well…"

She gestured toward the open office. "Right. I'm keeping you. Go on in. Make yourself at home. If you want privacy, just shut the door. I won't mind. If I need anything, I'll knock. Just promise you'll be careful. I almost never touch that computer. Jim gets really upset if he thinks I'm fiddling with his programs."

"Understood," Cody said.

Trudy Lynn noticed that not only was she babbling again, her hands were making exaggerated, fluttery motions to accent her words. That fit with the way the butterflies in her stomach were behaving. She'd been unnecessarily on edge all morning and it was beginning to rile her. What a ridiculous response to doing a simple favor. Surely, there was no need to be worried about Cody accidentally losing or corrupting important files, so why be nervous?

She solved her fidgeting problem by stuffing her hands into the pockets of her jeans. "Okay. Have at it. I'll go do some chores. See you later."

"Okay. Thanks."

Trudy Lynn paused to watch him turn and make his

way to the office. He did seem to be getting around a little better. Was he? Or was that just wishful thinking on her part?

Make that wishful *praying*. Cody Keringhoven had been in her prayers ever since Becky had told her he'd been hurt, and there was certainly nothing wrong with affirming a positive result. She didn't need the equivalent of thunder and lightning to convince her the Lord was working in Cody's life. She knew He was.

Though she still wasn't sure what part she might play in Cody's recovery, she was open to heavenly inspiration, just as long as it didn't require the kind of trust she'd once placed in Ned. Becoming involved with one overly controlling, pigheaded man had been an honest mistake. Falling for a second one who was carrying even more excess emotional baggage would be totally idiotic.

Besides, until she and Cody had recovered from the disappointments in their respective love lives, neither of them could count on thinking clearly. Entertaining the notion of becoming romantically involved again, let alone acting on it, scared her silly.

Trudy Lynn felt a sudden, overpowering urge to flee. She was outside, taking gulping breaths of fresh air, before she realized that no matter how much distance she put between herself and Cody Keringhoven, her tender-hearted sympathies would remain with him.

Okay. She could live with that. There was nothing wrong with well-placed compassion and concern. So what if she happened to like the man? That didn't automatically mean she was falling for him, did it? Of course not.

Letting her thoughts gel, Trudy Lynn began to smile and relax. She cared about a lot of people, her friends, her pastor, her employees, even the folks who rented canoes and campsites from her. Why not extend that same innocent sentiment to Cody? He might be grumpy at times but who wouldn't be, given his past? When he was in good spirits, he was a lot of fun to be around. There was nothing wrong with enjoying his company.

Satisfied with that logical conclusion, she skipped down the steps, feeling more lighthearted and more alive than she had for ages.

Cody was still seated in front of the computer monitor when Trudy Lynn returned and rapped on the doorjamb before poking her head in. "You busy?"

"No. Just finishing up. Am I in your way?"

"Not at all. As a matter of fact, maybe you can do me a favor. I called my insurance agent about the canoe that was damaged last night. She says she needs the date of purchase and the unit price before she can process my claim."

"How can I help?" Cody pushed back from the desk to give Trudy Lynn access when she approached.

Instead, she paused and held up her hands. "Oh, no. I'm not touching that thing. The last time I tried I messed up days and days of Jim's work."

"Don't you have the information you need on paper?"

She shrugged and quirked a lopsided smile. "Somewhere. Your guess is as good as mine. See those stacks of storage boxes over there? The white ones? Once Jim started putting all the data into the computer, I kind of quit keeping up any other files."

"Kind of?" Cody arched an eyebrow.

"Don't look at me like that. The stuff is in groups. I kept adding to a box till it was full, then started a new one. If I could remember approximately when we ordered those older canoes, I could probably locate the invoice. Eventually. Trouble is, the longer I take, the longer it'll be till I get any reimbursement. I thought, since you're good with computers, you could look it up for me."

"I'm not sure I want to. How big is your cousin?" Cody teased with a wry smile.

"Not big at all. He's a skinny teenager. Smart, but no muscleman like you."

Cody couldn't help feeling good about her description of him, especially when she began to blush. He laughed. "Muscleman? Thanks, I think."

"You know what I mean. You're taller, and… Oh, never mind."

To his delight, her rosy cheeks darkened even more. "Okay. Enough compliments," he said, carefully rolling the chair closer so it faced the desk. "Tell me how to access the accounts payable file and I'll see what I can find."

"I don't know." Trudy Lynn leaned over his shoulder to peer at the screen. "The thingie was already running when I got myself in trouble the last time."

"The *thingie?*" Cody chuckled low as he disconnected from the Internet and checked the listings of files. There were two with almost identical names. "Here you are. Which is it?"

"Beats me." She scowled. "One must be from last year. Open the one with the most recent activity and we'll work backward from there."

Cody checked dates. "This shows they've both been accessed in the past few days."

"Jim was probably looking for the insurance information on the other canoes that were ruined," she said. "Just pick either one."

"You could wait till your cousin comes back to work."

"I could," Trudy Lynn said, "but why dawdle when I have an expert sitting right here?" She pulled a face. "You are an expert, aren't you?"

"I won't accidentally erase anything, if that's what you're asking. I use a similar program to keep my investment portfolio. It's a pretty simple system once you get the hang of it."

"Not for me it isn't," she said with a smirk. "All machines hate me, even my vacuum cleaner. The only reason I can keep the ATV running is because Will uses it more than I do and it likes him. I think it's a guy thing."

"If you say so." Cody had been trying to open the chosen file and had failed. "What's your password?"

"Password? For what?"

"This file. It's password protected. Didn't you know that?"

"No." She laid a hand lightly on Cody's shoulder and leaned closer to read what was on the screen. "That's weird."

He forced himself to pay no heed to the warm touch

of her hand. It was harder to ignore the light, floral fragrance of her long brown hair as it neared his cheek.

"Not if Cousin Jim was worried you'd mess with the program again and cause him extra work," Cody said, fighting to concentrate on anything but his companion. "What's his last name? When's his birthday? Who's his current girlfriend?"

None of those answers proved to be the password so he began to try more eclectic terms. It wasn't until he used *weed* that he got a positive response. "Hmm. Not good. I'd rather he'd chosen something non-drug related."

"You don't know that's what that stands for."

"I have a pretty good idea," Cody argued, "unless you're going to tell me Jim is into horticulture."

"Unfortunately, no." Trudy Lynn squinted at the data. "Page down. Again. That can't be right. I didn't net nearly that much last month."

He looked up and noted her scowl. "Are you sure?"

"Positive."

"Okay. Let's print this page and check it against the other file."

"What good will that do?"

"Maybe none. Shall I go ahead and try it?"

"Sure." She shook her head, clearly confused. "Things were a lot simpler when I used to save my receipts in a shoe box and pay the bills myself."

"This system is more efficient," Cody told her.

"I suppose so. I just miss having a clear picture of how the business is doing. Looking at the printouts Jim gives me is not the same."

Cody clicked on the second file. To his surprise, it opened without difficulty. He leaned back in the chair and whistled softly.

"What?"

"Look at this. Is that more like what you think you earned last month?"

"Yes, but…"

"Wait a second," he said. "I want this on paper, too. Then we'll do some comparing."

"How will that help?"

Cody started the printer, then turned to study Trudy Lynn's expression. She was his sister's close friend. He couldn't imagine she'd be in on any scheme to defraud the government by keeping two sets of books in order to avoid paying income taxes. Although dishonest businesses did it all the time, or tried to, this woman didn't fit the pattern. She was too open. Too honest. Too clearly perplexed. Besides, if she'd been involved in cooking the books she wouldn't have invited an outsider like him to examine them.

Picking up the second printed sheet, Cody carefully compared it to the first, then laid them both facedown on the desk. He could see at a glance that part of the net difference was in the amount of hourly wage charged to her summer help.

"How much do you pay Anne and the other kids?" Cody asked.

Trudy Lynn quoted a figure far above what he'd seen on one of the sheets.

"How about Will?"

"I pay him about twice what the kids get. And I gave him a raise this year. Why?"

"One of these sets of books shows a good-sized increase. The other doesn't show nearly that much."

"So, one has to be from last year."

"Nope. Sorry." Cody could tell she was stunned. Good. That spoke well for her character. "I can't be positive without doing some serious math, but I suspect your cousin has been siphoning off cash for himself and charging it to other sources. The teens who work for you are only getting part of what you think you're paying them."

Cody displayed his findings and pointed out the discrepancies. "See? According to this posting, Will hasn't had a decent raise in at least two years, either."

"That's impossible!" Trudy Lynn snatched the papers from him, her glance darting back and forth between the two lists. Her eyes grew misty. "I can't believe it. There must be another explanation."

"I sincerely hope so," Cody said. "For your sake and for Jim's. Because if there isn't, you have more than one crime to worry about. You're a victim of embezzlement."

Trudy Lynn had ferried Cody back to his cabin and was sitting alone in her office, mulling over the morning's startling discovery, when her private phone rang. So few people knew that number she assumed it had to be a personal call. "Hello?"

"Ms. Brown? This is Billy Joe Potts, down at Serenity Realty, on the square. I brokered sales for several of your competitors last year. Remember?"

She tensed. "Vaguely."

"Well, Ms. Brown, I have great news for you. I've had an offer on your place that you won't be able to turn down. Isn't that amazing?"

The fine hairs at the nape of Trudy's neck were bristling. Her grip tightened on the receiver. "Amazing."

"Then you'll consider selling? That's wonderful! I knew you'd appreciate the chance to make a big profit. I'll bring the offer right over and get your signature. Say, in an hour?"

"No," Trudy Lynn said, masking her wariness as best she could. "I'm not free this afternoon. And tomorrow is Sunday. Why don't I stop by your office sometime Monday?"

"I don't mind working on the weekend."

"Well, I do. I'll be in church Sunday morning and evening. If you can't wait till Monday, perhaps we'd better just forget the whole thing."

"No, no! Don't...don't do that. Monday's fine."

His nervous, stammering protest was enough to prove to Trudy Lynn that something fishy was going on. She hung up and headed for Cody's cabin without hesitation.

As usual, she found him and his dog lounging on the porch. "Don't you ever go inside?" she asked pleasantly.

"Not if I can help it. At least not in nice weather like this."

"Well, since this is Arkansas, you might as well enjoy it while you can. Folks say our weather changes every twenty minutes." She joined him by sitting on the top step, as before. "Personally, I think that's an exaggeration. It usually takes at least thirty."

"I'll keep that in mind." He started to lower his propped-up leg.

"Sit still and be comfortable," Trudy Lynn said. "I can't stay. I just need a second opinion. Since you're the only one aware of the mess my finances are in right now, I thought you could give me the best advice."

"I'll try. What's up? Did you talk to your cousin?"

"Not yet. I did just get a call from a real estate agent, though. He says he's had an offer on this place."

"You told me you'd never sell."

"I still feel that way. But if I'm going to owe back taxes or be fined for filing erroneous tax returns or something like that, I don't know if I can afford to stay."

"I wouldn't make any rash decisions," Cody said. "I'd hate to see you give up when none of this mess was your fault. That's not like you. Where's that faith you keep talking about?"

"Sometimes it's hard to see God's plan. I have a tendency to try to second-guess Him."

"Must mean you're human."

"I guess so." She laced her fingers together around one knee and leaned back. "So, what do you think? Should I even bother talking to the real estate agent? He wants to see me Monday."

"Do you want to sell?"

"No. Of course not."

"Then turn down the offer, no matter how good it is. If you're meant to sell, there'll be another one."

"Trust God to work it out, you mean?" Trudy Lynn tilted her head back to grin up at him.

"I didn't say that."

"Yes, you did. But don't worry. I won't tell anybody. It'll be our secret, just you, me and Sailor." The Newf thumped his tail at the mention of his name.

"That's big of you."

The comical, cynical face Cody was making spurred her to chuckle quietly. "My pleasure. And speaking of things that are nice, how about letting me drive you to church tomorrow? I'm sure your sister would love to see you."

Cody huffed. "Yeah. Especially in her husband's church." He shrugged. "Oh well, why not? I want to talk to Logan, anyway."

"Not about the discrepancies in the books. Not yet," Trudy warned. "I don't want you to say anything to anybody till I've had a chance to hear Jim's side of it."

"I think you're wrong to wait. The sooner you get to the bottom of things, the less opportunity your cousin will have to erase the files and destroy the evidence."

"I've been thinking about that," she said. "Why would Jim want proof of his theft? It's nonsense to think he's that stupid."

"Not stupid," Cody replied, "overconfident and ego-tistical. He's sure he's smarter than anybody else and he wants a record of his accomplishments."

"Maybe he's keeping track because he means to return what he's taken."

Cody stared at her for a moment, then burst into laughter. "That's the most naive thing I've ever heard."

"Oh, yeah? Well, he deserves the benefit of the doubt, and I intend to give it to him."

"Because he's *kin,* as you all say around here?"

"Not entirely. I like to think I'd be that fair with anybody."

"What about the Randall kid? Were you positive he was a thief when you fired him?"

"Of course. Jim even saw..." Trudy realized what she was saying and broke off before Cody had a chance to interrupt. "Uh-oh. Jim again. You don't suppose...?"

"I don't know. But I do think I'd look into it if I were you. Just because a kid's family has problems, that doesn't mean he or she has to end up the same."

She scowled, studying Cody. His expression was innocent enough. However, if he'd been gossiping with Will there was no telling what tales he'd already heard about *her* parents.

Straightening and getting to her feet, she faced him. "Speaking of families, I want you to know my father was a fine man. He did the best he could for me and my mother. She was just fragile, that's all. It wasn't Daddy's fault."

"I'm sure it wasn't," Cody said.

If he'd shown any sign of puzzlement she would have stopped explaining. Since he appeared to know what she was referring to, she continued. "After Mama died, Daddy was never the same. I was barely in my teens but I did all I could to help him. I took over cooking, cleaning, paying the bills, everything. It was like he didn't care anymore. I know he couldn't stop blaming himself, wondering what more he could have done. In the end, I think it killed him, too."

"So, you've had to be strong for everybody else."

"Yes. I'm proud to say I'm nothing like my parents. I never give up."

Nodding, he spoke quietly and with compassion. "I understand. No wonder you kept insisting my client's drowning wasn't my fault. You knew what harboring guilt like that can do to a person."

"Yes. Firsthand."

Trudy Lynn was watching him closely, waiting for an argument, when she saw the clear blue of his eyes grow misty. She wasn't sure whether he was letting go of his misplaced blame or merely appreciating her opinion when he said, "Thank you," but she took it as a very good sign.

EIGHT

Sunday morning dawned bright and clear. Cody had been planning to catch Logan after church and ask him more about good old Cousin Jim. Now that he'd heard Trudy Lynn's sad tale of her childhood, he had a few questions for his sister, too.

Personal inquiries about his hostess were probably out of line, he realized, yet her revelation had touched him deeply. No wonder she was so determined to be self-reliant. At a time when she should have been enjoying childhood she'd been forced to step into a grown-up's shoes. Her skill and perseverance spoke well of her, yes, but there were still invisible scars.

Cody smiled as he dressed. Early success in an adult role had made Trudy Lynn the most hardheaded woman he'd ever met. Although he now understood some of the reasons for her stubbornness, she still drove him crazy. For instance when she'd charged the prowler with only a canoe paddle for defense!

He raked his fingers through his hair, venting his frustration. Much more excitement like that and he'd be turning gray before his time, as Sailor was starting to do around the muzzle.

One glance at the placid canine brought back Cody's smile. "You're going to be on your own this morning, boy. I'm going out. Think you can be good while I'm gone?"

The dog's head drooped. He laid his ears back and settled a pitiful gaze on his master.

"That's right. I'm leaving. And you're staying here. I want you to behave. I'll leave you plenty of food and water. Just don't break down any more doors, okay? Will wasn't real happy about fixing this one the last time."

His dog's expression made Cody shake his head and chuckle. "Now I know where the saying, hangdog-look, came from. That's the most miserable face you've ever made." He paused to ruffle the silky fur on the dog's ears. "Cheer up, fella. I'll bring you a treat. I promise."

He was still petting the dog when he heard a knock. Gathering up his crutches he called, "Come in. I'm ready."

Trudy Lynn eased the door open. The smile on her face grew to a grin when she saw him. "Morning."

"Good morning. I was just telling Sailor we'd bring him a treat. Will that be okay? I don't want to put you out, but I wouldn't want him to think I'd fib, either."

She giggled. "That's fine. We'll find something. Some of the stores are open on Sunday. And a few restaurants serve brunch after church, then close about two o'clock."

"They close early?" Cody joined her on the porch and secured the door. "Why?"

"Because it's Sunday, silly. The Sabbath."

"Ah, yes. Sunday in the Bible Belt. You weren't kidding about this part of the country being different, were you?"

"Nope." She led the way to her pickup and opened the door for him.

Cody scowled. "You don't have to baby me."

"Sorry. My mistake."

He watched her flounce around to the driver's side, her skirt swinging gracefully against her calves. If the green dress she'd ruined had actually been her favorite, this blue one deserved to be number two. It looked wonderful on her. Then again, everything she wore did.

Trudy Lynn slipped behind the wheel and peered over at him. "Well? Get a move on."

"Yes, ma'am." He positioned the crutches against the seat, parallel to his leg, and slammed the door. "Sorry I snapped at you."

"No problem. Sorry I was too nice. I'll do my best to be much meaner in the future."

"Thanks."

"You're welcome." She glanced at him as she drove out of the campground. "That's a nice jacket. You clean up pretty decent for a Californian."

"I was born in Illinois, remember?"

"I wouldn't tell that to too many folks till they get to know you better. I'm okay with it but some people think, *once a Yankee, always a Yankee.*"

"I'll keep that in mind."

"I doubt it." She laughed. "You tend to do things your way most of the time, no matter what."

Cody stared at her. "*I* tend to? What about you?"

"I can't help it if my way's the best way."

"Not always," he said firmly.

"Oh, yeah? Name one time when it wasn't."

His voice rumbled with emotion as he answered, "The time you charged an armed man and risked your life for a stupid canoe."

Remembering, she shivered in spite of herself.

The parking lot surrounding Serenity Chapel was already crowded when they arrived. Trudy Lynn considered stopping near the front doors so Cody wouldn't have to walk so far, then decided against it. She wasn't being mean, as she'd jokingly threatened, she was merely making him exercise. His mention of their misadventure while guarding the canoes had reminded her of how well he'd managed to get around when he'd been forced to. She didn't think for a minute that he was faking his disability and pain. But she did suspect he might be subconsciously punishing himself for the outcome of the original accident. If that were the case, it helped explain his refusal to continue physical therapy.

She found an empty space and parked. To Cody's credit, he didn't comment on how far they were from the entrance. By the time she'd gathered up her Bible and her purse, he was out of the truck, waiting.

"You've been here before, right?" she asked, leading the way.

"You know I have. This is where we first met."

"That's right. You were visiting Becky."

"Yes. You and Carol Sue sat in the pew behind my poor sister and me, giggling and whispering during the service."

"We did not!"

"Maybe not the whole time. But you two were sure enjoying yourselves."

"Why not? Church is a happy place," Trudy Lynn said.

"For you, maybe. Sometimes, I sit there feeling so much like an outsider I want to make a break for the door long before the sermon is over."

"Try to avoid making that kind of an exit this morning, will you? Becky and Logan would be embarrassed."

"Speaking of which, isn't that Logan standing inside, shaking hands?"

"Sure is. Go grab a pew for us. I'll join you in a few minutes. I need to pop into my Sunday school class first and explain why I wasn't there this morning so they won't worry."

Before Cody had time to ask if she'd missed the class on his account, Trudy Lynn had dashed off down the hall.

He approached Logan. "Good morning. Where's Becky?"

"Home," Logan said. "I think she's got a touch of the flu. We didn't give you our germs the other night, did we?"

"Nope. I'm healthy as a horse." He paused for a wry chuckle. "Of course, if I were a horse, they'd have shot me by now."

"How is your leg?"

"Sore." Cody shrugged. "But I didn't come here to

discuss my troubles. I need to have a private chat with you about my landlady."

"Trudy Lynn? Why? More vandalism?"

"I wish it were that simple," Cody said. "What else do you know about her cousin, Jim?"

"Nothing more than what I've already told you. That's public record so I wasn't violating a trust. Is Jim causing problems?"

"You have no idea." Cody lowered his voice and spoke aside. "I'm not going into any detail till you and I are alone, but it looks like he's been stealing from her."

"Really? Humph, that is a surprise. If I'd been asked to choose the person most likely to try to swindle her, I'd have picked her ex-boyfriend."

"Whoa. That's one suspect I hadn't considered." Cody was frowning. "I thought he was out of the picture."

"He's supposed to be. The thing is, my wife tells me Ned was never one to give up without a fight, even when they were kids. He had too much pride."

"Will says the guy dumped Trudy, not the other way around. Isn't that what happened?"

"In a manner of speaking. Once he'd graduated college, Ned let her know he wasn't coming back to town. When she refused to join him, he apparently insinuated she didn't measure up to his new standards of sophistication any more than Serenity did."

"Ouch. That had to hurt."

"If it did, you sure couldn't tell. She didn't even seem to care, which is why I wondered if Ned got his pride hurt and decided to cause trouble for her."

Logan paused to welcome some late arrivals, then said, "It's almost eleven. Come on. We can talk a little more on the way to my office."

By then, Cody was so involved in their conversation he'd have accompanied his brother-in-law if he'd had to crawl.

Logan stopped just inside his office door and checked his watch. "I can give you all of three minutes. What makes you think Jim is stealing?"

"Two sets of books, for starters. He's been doing all the accounts payable and giving Trudy's staff lower wages than she thought."

"He's pocketing the difference?"

"Looks like it. I didn't have time to go over all the records. Who knows what else he may have done? She insists she wants to talk to him before we go to the sheriff. If Jim finds out we're on to him, I'm afraid he'll panic and erase those files."

"A good tech can almost always get them back for you if you need them," Logan said. "That's a mistake lots of criminals make. They think data that doesn't show up in their computer's active memory is gone. Trust me. It isn't. It may be hard to access but it's still there."

"That's good to hear."

"So, tell me," Logan said with a knowing smile. "When did you start referring to yourself and our Ms. Trudy Brown as *we?*"

Exiting Miss Louella's Class for Extraordinary Ladies, Trudy Lynn was grinning. They'd teased her about coming to church with Cody that morning, as she'd expected. She didn't mind. The women in that class had the biggest, most loving hearts of any group she'd ever belonged to and it was their serious prayers she desired most.

Though she was loathe to admit it, especially to him, Cody had frightened her with his constant talk of danger. She'd never felt personally threatened before. Now, it was all she could do to make herself accompany Widget outside after dark. Having a spirit of fear was supposed to be wrong, so why was she unable to shake it?

Hurrying into the sanctuary, she paused at the rear. There weren't many tall, blond men in the congregation so she expected to spot Cody easily. Puzzled when she didn't see him, she started slowly down the center aisle, responding to greetings from fellow worshippers as she went.

She came upon Becky's aunt Effie and her new husband, Brother Fred, seated in the first row. "Hi. Have you seen Cody? We rode together."

"And you lost him?" Effie teased. "A big guy like that? My, my." She sobered. "How's he doing, anyway? We haven't heard much lately."

"Pretty well," Trudy Lynn said. "We expected to visit with Becky this morning. Have you seen her?"

"She's sick, I reckon. Nothin' else ever kept her out of church."

"That's too bad. Cody'll be disappointed. Assuming I ever locate him, that is."

"When you do, you'd best keep a close eye on him,"

the elderly woman warned. "Turning a handsome, single fella like that loose in here with all these unmarried ladies is like wavin' a pan of fudge under the nose of a gal who's been on a starvation diet. Anything might happen." She squeezed Fred's hand. "I always hold tight to this good catch of mine."

It warmed Trudy Lynn's heart to see the fond look the older couple exchanged. "I'll keep that in mind." Her already generous smile widened as she spotted her guest. "There's Cody. In the back. Safe and sound. If you talk to Becky, tell her I asked about her. I'll phone her later."

"Y'all could sit down here by us," Effie suggested. "There's plenty of room."

"I know. But it looks like Cody's having a little trouble balancing on the sloping aisle. We'll visit after the service, okay?"

Trudy Lynn didn't wait for an answer. She quickly joined Cody and motioned to an empty space in the back. "I was just talking to Effie and Brother Fred."

"Do you want to go sit with them?"

"That's not necessary. I said we'd talk later." Entering the pew, she left room for Cody and his crutches. When he was comfortably seated she added, "I guess Becky's sick this morning."

"That's what Logan said."

"You had a chance to talk with him? You didn't mention those problems we found, did you?"

"I certainly did."

Trudy Lynn was irritated. "I told you I wanted to

speak to Jim before we said anything to anybody. I should have known you wouldn't listen to me."

"I listened. Calm down and think for a second. Logan was already aware of some of Jim's problems and he also has a professional background. There was no reason to keep our suspicions from him. We need his advice."

Trudy Lynn pulled a face. She had no plausible grounds to disagree. "Okay. I suppose you're right. *This* time. So, tell me. What did Logan have to say?"

"Not to worry about the files being erased, among other things."

"What other things?" Scowling, she tried to be patient. Expecting a man to make sense was problematical. Getting this one to reveal anything was like waiting for Widget to spit out a grasshopper—whatever parts did finally show up, it probably wasn't going to be the whole insect.

Cody leaned closer. He lowered his voice to ask, "What are the chances your ex-boyfriend could be our vandal?" She drew back and scowled.

"Ned? That's ridiculous."

"Is it? Why?"

"Because."

"That's not a very good reason."

"It's good enough for me. Ned insisted nothing would ever make him set foot in this hick town again and I believed him. I'm sure that opinion extends to my campground. He never did like the place."

"He's a fool," Cody said flatly.

Trudy Lynn's cheeks warmed. No wonder it was so

hard to stay upset with this impossible man. Every time he made her mad he seemed to follow up with something so endearing, so unexpected, it instantly negated her annoyance.

She smiled. "What a nice thing to say. I'm glad you appreciate the beauty of this area. I love it here."

The service was starting, giving Cody barely enough time to cup his hand around his mouth and add, "I wasn't referring to the real estate."

To Trudy Lynn's credit she managed to listen to most of Logan's sermon, although if anyone had asked her, she knew she couldn't have recalled its content. She figured she was doing well to accompany Cody out the door afterward without grinning so broadly her cheek muscles cramped.

They chatted briefly with Effie and Fred before bidding them goodbye and starting for the parking lot. Trudy Lynn stopped in surprise when she saw her supposedly nefarious cousin leaning against the side of her pickup truck. His nonchalant pose made her wary. Jim never relaxed. His manner was usually comparable to that of a nervous hummingbird. Seeing him standing so quietly, obviously waiting for her, was a bit unnerving.

She would have reached for Cody's arm if his crutches hadn't been in the way. Instead, she put her hand lightly on his shoulder. "See that guy by the truck? That's Jim. I wonder what he wants." She shuddered. "You don't think Brother Logan called him, do you?"

"Not for a minute. Logan takes his job too seriously.

He'd never betray a confidence." Cody started forward. "Come on. It's high time I met your cousin."

Trudy Lynn had to hurry to keep up. She reached the truck at the same time Cody did and forced a smile. "Hi, Jim. I'd like you to meet Cody Keringhoven. He's Becky's brother."

"I heard you'd taken in a stray." The wiry teen snorted, obviously passing judgment.

Before Trudy Lynn could object to Jim's lack of respect, Cody said, "I'm not freeloading, if that's what you're thinking. I'm working for my keep."

Jim eyed him up and down. "Oh, yeah? Doin' what?"

"Looking out for prowlers, to start with," Cody said evenly. "I'm also pretty good at bookkeeping."

"Hey! That's my job," Jim blurted, abandoning his lackadaisical facade.

Trudy Lynn could tell how worried the younger man was. Good. Let him sweat. If they'd made a mistake and Jim was innocent of the suspected theft, she'd apologize. Unfortunately, it didn't look as if she was going to have to. Jim was giving a perfect impression of a naughty kid who'd been caught with his hand in the cookie jar. *Her* cookie jar. And she wasn't ready to forgive what he'd already done to her staff. The worst part was, she couldn't afford to make it up to them retroactively.

"Those books are mine," Trudy Lynn said. "I can look at them anytime I want to. Right?"

"Sure." Jim's bony shoulders twitched. "No problem. I'll print you out whatever you want."

"From which file?" she asked without smiling.

Her cousin's glance darted to Cody. When he began to glare at the man, any lingering doubt Trudy Lynn had was swept away. Jim was as guilty as if he'd robbed her at gunpoint. That would have been hard enough to accept coming from a stranger. This boy was *family*.

Saddened, she said, "We haven't gone to the sheriff, Jimmy. Not yet. But we will if you don't have a *very* good explanation for what you did."

"You owed me the money," he said, as if that made his thievery acceptable.

"I gave you as much as I could afford. You knew what the job paid when you took it."

"Yeah. I knew." He snorted derisively. "I knew a lot of other stuff, too. You don't have a clue."

"I want to understand." She gently laid her hand on his thin forearm and felt it tremble. "Don't be afraid."

Jim jerked free. "I ain't afraid of nothin'."

"Then calm down and come back to the office with us. I want you to show Mr. Keringhoven everything— all the duplicate files you set up. Then we'll talk. I'm sure we can work something out so you won't have to go to jail."

"Yeah, sure." He was backing away. "Later."

Trudy Lynn stood beside Cody and watched the teen cut across the lawn to the street. She sighed. "Do you think he'll show up?"

Cody shook his head. "Not in a million years."

NINE

That Sunday afternoon had begun sultry and ended wet, thanks to a surprise storm. The rain didn't have to last long to impress Cody. Drops as big as quarters were driven horizontal by a gale that looked as if it was strong enough to snap the tops off the trees. He waited it out in the camp store with Trudy Lynn while Anna tended to the few customers daring enough to brave the deluge.

"Does it always come down like this?" Cody asked.

Trudy Lynn laughed. "No. Sometimes it's worse. Our storms are very unpredictable. This is the kind of weather that can spawn tornadoes, too."

"Terrific. And for this I left California?"

"Why did you leave, anyway?"

"Lots of reasons."

"One of them wouldn't happen to be similar to my story about Ned, would it?"

"Maybe. I haven't met Ned so I can't judge his motives. I imagine Stephanie was prettier, though."

To his chagrin, he saw the twinkle fade from Trudy's eyes. "All her beauty was on the outside," Cody quickly explained. "There was a callous element to her personality that I never saw till I wound up on crutches."

"I'm sorry."

He smiled. "I used to be sorry, too. Now, I'm glad I found out before it was too late. When—if—I ever do decide to get married, I intend for it to last the rest of my life." He raised an eyebrow. "Admit it. Haven't you felt the same kind of relief about Ned?"

"Truthfully? Yes. I can't picture myself tagging along after him and pretending I like being in the city. Even if I could have managed to please him temporarily, I'd eventually have resented him for taking me away from all this." She swept her arm in a wide arc. "I belong here the same way those oaks and sycamores belong in the forest. Or the Spring River belongs in its banks. They just do."

Cody nodded. "I know exactly what you mean. I felt the same about the Tuolumne."

"Felt? Past tense? I thought you were looking forward to going back there as soon as you were able."

"Not anymore." He shrugged. "I've accepted my limitations."

"You can still enjoy being on the water. How about going canoeing with me as soon as the weather clears?"

"No thanks."

"Why not? It would do you good to get out. Our river may not be as exciting as you're used to but it's not boring, either. There's lots to see—birds, deer, all kinds of wildlife."

"I said, *no*."

Cody didn't like the way Trudy Lynn was studying

his face, trying to read him. It was embarrassing to admit, even to himself, how his stomach churned every time he thought about getting back into a boat. Any boat. On any watercourse. The last thing he was going to do was confess those irrational feelings and open himself to ridicule. He gritted his teeth. Worse than that, Trudy Lynn might decide to help him overcome his hang-ups, with or without his consent.

Moments later, she said, "Fine," as if it didn't matter.

"I couldn't even get into a canoe with this brace on my knee," he said, hoping to soothe her bruised pride. "Maybe later." *And maybe never.*

"Okay. If you decide you want to take out one of my canoes by yourself, just tell Will. He'll fix you up."

Cody took her hand. To his relief, she didn't resist his easy grasp. "I'm not turning down your offer because I don't want to ride with you, Trudy Lynn. I'm turning it down because…" Her clear, trusting gaze unnerved him. "Just because I don't want to go, okay?"

"Okay." She pulled her hand free, got to her feet and peered out the window. "It's still raining. Looks like that terrible wind has eased, though, so we can probably quit worrying about getting hit by falling limbs. It's safe enough to drive you on home. Let's go."

Cody's conscience was doing backflips. If he voiced his apprehension about boating, he'd have to admit to the possibility it might never go away. Plus, he'd have to continue to face Trudy Lynn, an extraordinary woman who was as fearless as any man he'd ever met. That notion didn't set well in his already churning gut.

Mulling over his predicament, it occurred to Cody that he cared too much what his hostess thought of him. Way too much. In the space of a few days, staying in her good graces and ensuring her welfare had become the most important goals in his life. It was nice to know he could accomplish that by relying on his brain, even if his knee never healed properly. And he wouldn't starve. His investments would see to that. So why was he so downhearted?

Because I never appreciated what I had before, he decided. And now there was no way to reclaim it.

Watching Trudy Lynn lead the way to her truck, he paused on the porch and began to smile. It might be too late to be grateful for his past but it wasn't too late to give thanks for the present. For being here. For being dragged into the intrigue surrounding his hostess.

Cody *was* grateful. Sincerely so. Yet his heart held back from actually acknowledging the benevolent influence of a higher power. Although the idea of a universal God did make sense, he still doubted any deity cared for him personally or noticed if he stumbled. That premise was okay for women and children. It was too far-fetched for him.

Trudy Lynn had dropped Cody in front of his cabin, then returned to the main lodge to transmit her grocery order by phone to the computer at the warehouse which supplied her store. She'd just finished when Will thumped up the steps in his rubber boots and flung open the door. He was dripping rainwater and panting.

His demeanor was enough to alert her. "What's wrong? More vandalism? Surely not on a Sunday."

"No, ma'am." The old man mopped his wet face with his hands. "It's worse."

"What could be worse?"

"Plenty. We're missin' a canoe."

"That's not too unusual after a storm like the one we just had. The rain probably floated it off. Don't get yourself in a tizzy. I'm sure it didn't go far."

"This one did," Will said, still breathless. "Jim took it. Farley saw him push off and head downriver, right as the rain was commencin'."

"Then we'll pick him up at one of the landings as soon as he calls. If he doesn't phone before I leave for services tonight, wait till I get back. I want to be the one who goes and gets him."

"You ain't thinkin' of goin' by yourself, are ya?"

She hadn't given it a lot of thought. "Why not?"

"I don't like it," Will said, scowling. "That boy ain't been actin' right for months. Mark my words, he's up to something. I wouldn't trust him no farther than I could throw him. Maybe not that far."

"If you were so worried, why didn't you tell me?"

"Because he's your kin."

"The only thing Jim and I have in common is our ancestors and I'm about ready to disown him. What, exactly, has he done to make you suspicious?"

"Sneakin' around for one thing. Seems like he's always turning up. For a while there I thought he was spyin' on me, checkin' to see if I was workin' hard enough."

"What else?"

"Those friends of his. Bunch of no-goods if I ever seen 'em. Always hangin' around and moochin' free rides. If I had a nickel for every time he let one of his buddies take a canoe without payin', I'd be a rich man."

"Didn't you say something to him about it?"

"Sure did," Will told her with pride. "I took him aside and gave him what for."

"And?" Trudy Lynn was beginning to think Will would never finish his story to her satisfaction.

"And, he cussed at me. Said you gave him permission. If I'd of run to you about it after that, I'd of sounded as spoiled as he is. It's none of my business if you want to let him treat his friends."

"Only I never said he could." The more she probed, the worse Jim's sins got. What else was waiting to be uncovered?

Will looked apologetic. "I'm terribly sorry, Miz Brown. I shoulda known."

"Don't worry about it. You're not the only one who was fooled. Is that all Jim did?"

"All that I know of. 'Course, that don't mean there ain't more. What're you goin' to do? Wait him out?"

"For now." She nodded, thoughtful. "If we don't hear from him by nightfall, we'll call the sheriff and report the canoe stolen."

"Jim'll be fit to be tied."

"Good. He needs shaking up. I wouldn't be doing him any favors if I let him get away with this."

The truth of that statement entered her subconscious

and began to bounce around as Widget's favorite tennis ball had done the time it had accidentally ended up in the clothes dryer. Maybe Jim did need to be forced to face his misdeeds and right them—before she granted him forgiveness. There was a lot to be said for standing up and taking your medicine, even if it was hard to swallow.

Like Cody needs to do, she thought. Jim wasn't the only one who should be made to face facts. In a way, Cody's task was more difficult. His problems had resulted from an accident, while the origin of Jim's was his own missteps.

Which is probably why Cody blames God, Trudy Lynn mused. That wasn't as terrible as she'd first imagined. In his misplaced anger he was at least acknowledging a basic belief in the Lord. That was a start. She knew she couldn't argue him into a renewal of his faith, though the urge to try was strong. Too bad Christianity wasn't catching like the common cold or genetic like his light-colored hair.

Will was still standing by, waiting for orders, when her thoughts returned to the problem at hand. Wherever her cousin was, chances were good he was okay. The storm had arisen fairly suddenly but Jim was a native of Arkansas so he knew how severe the weather could get. Surely, he'd have beached the canoe and waited it out when the heaviest rain had begun. He'd have had to. Seeing where he was going and piloting the boat in the midst of such a deluge would have been impossible.

"Okay, Will," she said. "I'll stay close to the phones in case Jim calls. You go ask Farley if he mentioned anything that may give us a clue to where he was headed."

"Yes, ma'am. You want me to tell Mr. Cody what's goin' on, too?"

The old man's keen perception amused and embarrassed her. "Yes. You can tell Cody. He's going to be helping me in the office for a while so he should be kept informed about camp business."

"You fire ol' Jim?"

"Not yet," Trudy Lynn said, "but I'm going to."

"What'll his grandma Earlene say?"

"I doubt she'll be too surprised. She's had eighteen years of watching after him while his mama worked." Trudy Lynn began to smile. "I don't suppose you'd like to drop by Earlene's place and tell her for me, would you?"

"Who? Me?"

To her delight, the old man's face reddened. "Yes, you. Word around town is, you've been goin' to church with her on the Sunday evenings you don't have to work."

"I mighta gone a few times."

"Uh-huh. Well, as soon as I can get things squared away here, you'll have every Sunday off. Tell Earlene that for me when you see her, too."

"I didn't say I was goin'."

"You're going. Consider it an order. I'd rather have you break it to her about Jim than have to do it myself."

"In that case, I think you'd best pass the word to Mr. Cody." Will began to grin. "If I have to run into town and break the bad news to Earlene, it could take me hours, by the time I get her settled down and all."

Laughing softly, Trudy Lynn assented. "I suppose that's fair. I'll go tell Cody and you go tell Earlene."

Pausing, she shook her head. "But don't think I'm not wise to you, old man. You can pretend you're not interested in her all you want. You don't fool me one bit."

Will was chuckling when he answered, "You don't fool me, either, missy."

If Cody was surprised by Trudy Lynn's visit he didn't show it. He joined her on the porch and dried the pressed-metal chairs with a towel before offering her one. That show of hospitality didn't impress her nearly as much as the fact he was getting around nicely with the aid of a cane he'd borrowed from Will.

"Jim's gone," she said, sinking into the closest chair with a sigh. The cool dampness felt good.

Cody lowered himself into the other chair. "I figured he'd run. So, what now?"

"We wait. Since he stole a canoe instead of taking the ATV, his trail will be easy to follow. Even if he decides to beach the boat downriver and take off on foot his options are limited. When he gets tired of hanging out in the woods with the ticks and chiggers he'll come back. I know Jim. He won't rough it for long. He's spoiled rotten."

"We have ticks in northern California," Cody said. "Tell me what a chigger looks like so I can avoid them, too. I've heard they really make you itch."

Trudy Lynn gave him a lopsided smile. "*Oh,* yeah. If you ever find one big enough to see, I'd like to take a peek, too. The first inkling you'll have that you've been bitten is a little red spot, usually somewhere near your ankles. I put home remedies on my chigger bites, not that anything works very well. You kind of have to tough it out till the itching finally stops."

"How long does that take?"

"Well," she drawled, smile spreading, "I'm usually through scratching my summer bites by Christmas."

"No wonder Sailor's been acting uncomfortable. We forgot to buy him a flea collar."

"Or two. I left Widget home so he wouldn't traumatize your gentle giant again. Where is he, anyway?"

"Inside. Sleeping," Cody said. "I've been thinking."

"*That's* a good sign."

"Be serious and let me finish, will you?"

"Sorry." She made a comical face to show she was far from being intimidated.

"Did Widget like Jim?"

"Not particularly," Trudy Lynn said.

"I wish Sailor had met him."

"Why? Is he out of tasty snacks or chew toys?"

Cody gave a wry chuckle. "No. But he is intuitive, especially about people he doesn't already know. I've seen it before. He's the best judge of character I've ever met."

"And he loved me the minute he saw me!"

"You were covered in gravy at the time. That's hardly a fair test."

"True. He did seem to like me after that, too, didn't he?"

"Yes." Cody blessed her with a grin. "He liked you. I told you he was a great judge of character."

Her cheeks grew rosy. "Thanks. Widget told me he liked you, too." It pleased her when that far-fetched comment made Cody laugh.

"So," he said a moment later, "what's Plan B? Are you going to call the cops on Jim or let him off?"

"I'm not going to let him get away with stealing, if that's what you mean. It isn't just me he cheated, it's my employees. Too bad none of them questioned their wages."

"Maybe they did and Jim gave them some lame excuse."

Trudy Lynn had already considered that probability. When all this was over and things were back to normal, she intended to give as many raises as her budget would allow, even if it meant no new equipment for several seasons.

She nodded in agreement. "That's entirely possible. I don't want to discuss it with the kids until I know for sure how much damage has been done, but I may tell Will. He'll understand."

"Because he's been on both sides of the law?"

"Of course not!" Trudy Lynn stared at Cody as if he'd just delivered a personal insult. "Will's my friend. I trust him, even if you don't."

"I'm sorry if I offended you," Cody said evenly. "You asked for my help solving your mystery and I've been doing my best to give it. If you'd rather deal with fairy tales than hear the truth, I'll stop."

"I didn't mean that."

"Then what did you mean?"

Good question. She sighed. Everything was getting too complicated. Not only had she been disappointed to learn negative aspects regarding people close to her, she was having to come to grips with her own vacillating point of view on a minute-by-minute basis. Was she or wasn't she interested in developing a personal relationship with Cody Keringhoven? And if she was, how did he feel about it? Given the severity of her other tribulations, that should have been the least of her worries, yet she couldn't help constantly wondering.

Clearly, Cody was waiting for an answer. "I don't know what I meant," Trudy Lynn said. "This whole business has me so bumfuzzled—confused—I don't even make sense to myself. And believe me, I've been talking myself silly."

"I don't doubt that."

It was a relief to see his good humor returning, even though she was once again the focus of his taunt. "I do not talk too much."

"Oh?" He glanced at his watch. "I've been timing you. The longest you can go without having to say something is about twenty seconds."

"That's ridiculous."

"Is it? Try keeping still."

The man was exasperating. Did he really expect her to believe she couldn't stop talking, any time she wanted, for as long as she wanted? Of course she could. She pressed her lips together and waited. And waited. Finally, her patience was at an end.

"All right. How was that? Can I talk now?"

Cody was laughing. "Nineteen seconds. You just proved my point."

Waving her hands like a demented butterfly caught in a whirlwind, she got to her feet and faced him. "Oh, who cares? I'm going to go back to the office and see if Jim has called from one of the landings downriver. If he hasn't, I'm going to drive the usual route and check each one. Do you want to come along or are you afraid to be cooped up in a truck with somebody who chatters like I do?"

"I think I can stand it," Cody said. "Give me a few minutes to be sure Sailor's going to be all right while I'm gone."

"Fine. I'll be right back."

Hurrying away, Trudy Lynn was struck by the fact she was suddenly so elated she wanted to jump for joy. Her life was falling apart, her business might go down the tubes, she still hadn't figured out who was trying to ruin her new canoes, and her cousin had absconded after embezzling who-knows-how-much from her accounts, yet she was ecstatic to the point of being giddy.

There could be only one reason for that, she admitted ruefully. Like it or not, her spirits were up because she and Cody were about to spend more time together.

TEN

Cody could have predicted they wouldn't find any trace of Jim no matter how many landings and byways they searched. Night was fast approaching when Trudy Lynn voiced the same conclusion. "I guess we should give up and go home."

"Guess so." Cody tried to sound supportive. "You've done all you can. It's probably time to involve the law."

"I know." She sighed heavily. "I kept hoping. We'll stop at the sheriff's office when we go through Serenity. I'd rather talk to him in person than by phone."

"On Sunday night?"

She blinked rapidly and peered at the digital clock on her dash. "Oh, no. We've missed church. I was so involved in looking for Jim I let the time slip by."

"That's okay. Why don't we stop at Becky and Logan's and tell them what's been going on? I'd like to see how she's feeling, anyway. Do you think they'd be home by now?"

"Undoubtedly, even if they stopped for ice cream. Evening services don't last all that long."

Cody's stomach growled. "Ice cream? Sounds good. I didn't eat lunch."

"You mean, *dinner.* Around here, dinner is served right after church, around noon. Supper is the late meal."

"No lunch?"

"Nope."

"How—Southern." He'd been going to say something less genteel but changed his mind. After the way his hostess had bristled when he'd reminded her of Will's prison record, he'd decided to choose his words more carefully in future conversations. Judging by her amiable reaction to his latest efforts to subdue his candor, he'd succeeded.

Turning slightly to stretch his stiff knee, Cody draped his left arm across the back of the seat between them and studied Trudy Lynn's profile as she drove. It was amazing how her freshness and natural beauty remained so compelling despite the trying day she'd had.

The driver's side window was partially open and the wind was lifting wisps of her long, silky hair. It feathered against his forearm like butterfly wings. He knew he should move away. And he would. He just didn't see any rush.

Trudy Lynn shot him a bemused glance. "What?"

"Ice cream," Cody said, seizing on the first excuse that came to mind. "I'll buy. I'm starving."

"I thought you wanted to go see your sister."

"Let her get her own ice cream," he joked. "I never treat more than one pretty lady at a time." The glib words were out of his mouth before he fully realized what he'd said. There was no hope that Trudy Lynn had missed the inference. Her cheeks were flaming. Anything he said now would only make matters worse.

Hunkering down in the seat and facing forward, arms folded across his chest, Cody used the remaining miles to try to figure out how he'd turned into such a blithering idiot in just a short few days.

Trudy Lynn left Cody talking with Logan and followed Becky into the kitchen. "How are you feeling?" she asked.

"Mostly okay," her friend said. "It comes and goes. I can be fine one minute and woozy the next."

"Then sit down and let me make the coffee," Trudy Lynn said. "I wanted to get you alone, anyway."

"Uh-oh. Sounds serious. More trouble?"

"I hope not." She busied herself with the coffeemaker while she organized her thoughts. "I'm really starting to like your brother."

"That's *bad?*"

"It could be. We hardly know each other."

"How does he feel about it?"

Trudy Lynn's eyes widened. "I don't know. I don't want to know. We're both on the rebound. It's way too soon for either of us to be having any serious ideas."

"Then what's the problem?"

"I haven't been leading him on. At least I don't think I have. But on the way over here he said I was pretty."

"How awful. I'll have Logan tell him to mind his manners."

"Stop teasing. It's hard to remember exactly what Cody said and how he said it."

"Try." Becky leaned her elbows on the table, rested her chin in her hands and grinned knowingly.

"And stop staring at me like that. I happen to *like* the man. I never said I was falling in love or anything."

"Perish the thought. Go on. Protest as much as you want if you think it'll help. I'm a pastor's wife. You'd be amazed at the secrets people tell me."

Trudy Lynn was adamant. "There's no secret. Nothing. I'm probably imagining things. Cody and I were talking about how you and Logan sometimes go get ice cream after evening services. Cody said he was hungry and offered to pay if I'd stop for ice cream for us."

"So far, so good. That all made sense."

"I know. But then, he said you should get your own ice cream because he only treats one pretty lady at a time. I know he was just kidding around. I suppose I shouldn't take it so seriously."

Becky laughed softly. "Well, well. He stuck his foot in it that time, didn't he?"

"What do you mean?"

"Reason it out, honey. I'm not only married, I'm his sister, so that leaves only one pretty, available lady. You."

"We're *not* on a date," Trudy Lynn insisted. "Nothing like it. We've been driving around looking for Jim that's all." She sobered and sighed. "I suppose I might as well tell you. You'll hear the gossip soon enough. Jim's been embezzling from me. When I confronted him, he promised to come to the office and talk. Instead, he took a canoe and disappeared downriver."

Becky whistled. "Wow. What're you going to do now?"

"Cody's getting Logan's advice, for starters. Then, I guess we'll have to call the sheriff."

"I should hope so. Is there anything I can do to help?"

"No. Thanks anyway." Trudy Lynn began frowning. "Except maybe tell me why your coffeemaker isn't starting to drip. I filled it with fresh water."

Laughing, her friend stood and reached across the counter. She held the end of a brown cord in front of her face and wiggled it as she said, "I think it works better if you plug it in. Always has for me."

If Trudy Lynn had envisioned the turmoil and confusion that would descend upon her formerly peaceful camp as a result of Jim's vanishing act, she might have considered writing off the monetary loss after all.

The local police had been the only ones involved in the search to begin with. After they'd located a bloody life vest and splintered paddle, however, they'd called in a state investigative team which had come equipped with its own mobile command center and full staff. That team's activation caught the attention of the Arkansas newspapers, followed by wider distribution on the newswires. Soon, a number of reporters from nearby towns began to set up camp in Serenity.

Trudy Lynn didn't mind the extra business for her store and cabins. What disturbed her was the cancellations from her regular customers. She was just hanging up the receiver after another disappointing conversation when Cody entered the office.

"Hi. Any news?"

Trudy Lynn shook her head and gestured toward the phone. "Not anything good. That was the Millers. They've had reservations since they were here last summer. Suddenly they've changed their minds. Lots of my usual campers aren't coming this year."

"Because of what happened to Jim?"

"Yes. Everybody's positive he's been murdered or come to some equally horrible end." She scowled and pursed her lips. "If you ask me, he faked his disappearance. Anything to get out of being held responsible for his crimes."

"That's highly possible," Cody said. "But if he intended to hide, he sure went about it the wrong way. With all these people looking for him, one of them is bound to turn up a clue. It's only a matter of time." He approached and reached for Trudy Lynn's hand before he went on. "Unless Jim really has met with foul play. There is that possibility. The sheriff tells me some of your cousin's friends have bad reputations."

Head bowed, she stared at the gentle way Cody was holding her hand and stroking his thumb over her knuckles. It was the kind of unspoken comfort she'd craved and never received after her mother's death. Even later, when she'd begun to seriously consider spending the rest of her life with Ned, he'd never touched her with quiet compassion the way Cody had.

"I wish I'd never hired Jim," she said softly. "Earlene

convinced me to give him a chance. She's Jim's maternal grandmother. She's been a better parent to him than his mom ever thought of being."

"What about his father?"

"Long gone."

"Too bad. I know what it's like to grow up in a one-parent home. Dad did his best for me but it still wasn't as good as it could have been with a mother in the house, especially when I was younger."

"I know what you mean." Trudy Lynn felt instantly bereft when Cody released her hand and stepped back.

"Tell you what," he said. "Let's check all the landings again and do our own snooping. It'll be better than sitting here stewing over the lack of progress the professionals are making."

"Great idea. We can take a canoe. The weather's perfect for it. And I need a break. You can hardly hear yourself think in the store or on the porch with all the police activity."

Although she'd started toward the outer door, Cody hadn't budged. She looked back. "Aren't you coming?"

"I'll take a rain check."

"Why? This was your idea."

"I meant we could drive."

"What's the difference?" She saw him glance down at his knee. "Don't worry. You'll be able to get into a canoe. I'll be there if you need help."

"No, thanks."

Puzzled, she tried to read his closed expression. If she didn't know how daring he'd been before, she might suspect he was afraid. That was impossible of course. Cody was used to taking chances. A little canoe ride on a peacefully flowing river wouldn't scare him one bit. Therefore, the only possible conclusion was that he didn't want her company. So much for the silly notion the man was growing fond of her.

Pride came to her rescue. She lifted her chin and squared her shoulders. "Okay. Have it your way. I should relieve Anna for her afternoon break instead of going on a wild-goose chase, anyway. I may not have a business left when all this is over, but we're sure raking in the money right now. Better make the most of it."

"Right. Guess I'll take Sailor for a swim. It beats bathing him in the bathtub."

"And it's easier on the plumbing," Trudy Lynn said. "I've had clogged sinks in two of the cabins since the reporters showed up. I suspect they forget we don't have garbage disposals so they dump food scraps down the drain."

"I'll mention it to them for you."

"That won't be necessary."

"It's no bother. Glad to do it."

Trudy Lynn's hands fisted on her hips. "I said, it won't be necessary. I've already handled it."

"Who put the burr under *your* saddle, lady?"

"Nobody. I appreciate your offer, but…"

"But?"

"I was running this place all by myself before you came to Serenity. Nothing has changed. I can still do it."

"I never said you couldn't. While I was delivering my

speech about the cabin sinks, I thought I'd try to get the reporters talking, maybe piece together some clues."

"Good idea. I'll do that as soon as Anna gets back from her break. Now, if you'll excuse me?"

The dumbfounded expression on Cody's face reminded Trudy Lynn of the time she'd stood up to him at Becky's. Back then, he'd been the grumpy one. This time, it was she who had set the strident tone of their exchange. She was already penitent. How could she hope to influence Cody for the good if she didn't treat him with civility? Moreover, the example she was setting of loving Christian behavior was sorely lacking.

She knew she should apologize. The trick was deciding what to say. In this case, blurting out the plain truth would be embarrassing to all concerned. She could just picture Cody's astonishment if she told him, "I was short-tempered because I apparently have a crush on you and you hurt my feelings when you wouldn't go for a canoe ride with me." Talk about a lame excuse for being uppity! Explained that way, her reaction was on a par with the temper tantrum of a spoiled brat. That comparison made her shudder.

Okay, so she wasn't perfect. At least she kept trying to be kinder and more understanding. Later, when she'd cooled off and was thinking clearly, she'd seek out Cody and tell him she was sorry she'd snapped at him. Given the tense atmosphere in the camp, he'd probably be able to accept that excuse for her being on edge. As long as he didn't insist she explain further, she'd be satisfied.

* * *

The afternoon passed in a blur. Trudy Lynn had long ago lost count of how many soft drinks, candy bars and bags of ice she'd sold. Doing an inventory and ordering another truckload of supplies midweek was going to be a top priority.

First, however, she was going to do herself a favor and escape. Her urge to grab a canoe and get away from the chaos in camp had been building ever since she'd suggested the trip to Cody. Just because he didn't want to accompany her didn't mean she had to sit there and go quietly nuts while the nosy reporters and concerned searchers looked at her askance, as if she might hold the answers to what had become of Jim.

The only person she confided in was Will. Trudy Lynn slipped down to the dock and took the old man aside. "I'm going downriver. If anybody asks, just tell them I stepped out for a few minutes."

"I don't know if this is such a good idea," Will said as he helped her launch a red canoe. "Jim might be out there, waitin' for somebody to drift by alone so's he can steal their boat or something."

"He'd have to catch me, first. You know I'm a wiz with a paddle."

Will started to mutter under his breath. She couldn't help teasing him. "One word about women being weak and I'll bean you with my purse. A blow like that could be fatal."

"That's 'cause it's full of all that heavy money you've been takin' in. Never knew you to carry a purse on the river, though, so I'll take my chances. Just see *you* don't take any."

"I won't. I plan to drift awhile, calm down and try to get my head on straight. This whole experience with Jim has made me way too irritable."

"You ought to take that Cody fella with you."

"I invited him. He turned me down."

The old man shrugged. "Okay. You're the boss. Where do you want me to send the van?"

"I don't know. I haven't decided how far I'll go yet." She patted her pocket. "I have my cell phone. I'll call after I land and tell you where to pick me up.

"Before nightfall?"

Chuckling, she nodded. "Yes, *Papa.* Before the sun goes down. I promise." A person in a familiar, bright blue jacket caught her eye. "Uh-oh. One of those stubborn reporters I've been avoiding is headed this way. Gotta go. Don't worry. I'll be fine. And don't let anybody follow me." She pointed. "Especially not her."

"Yes, ma'am."

Pushing off, Trudy Lynn paddled furiously. She hadn't believed there was any limit to her capacity for hospitality until recently. Now, she knew otherwise. All she wanted was for everybody to pack up and go home. Well, *almost* everybody. She wouldn't mind if Cody Keringhoven stayed a while longer.

Cody again, she mused. *Always Cody.*

As her paddle slid silently into the water with hardly a ripple she realized that Cody had slipped into her mind, into her heart, as effortlessly as that smooth paddle bisected the clear, cold water. He was already an integral part of her thoughts. And, like the river that flowed into the emptiness left by the retreating paddle and obliterated all sign of its passing, she couldn't look back and see how it had happened.

Cody finished turning the tables on the reporters, in spite of Trudy Lynn's admonition against it, and headed for the little store to report what he'd learned. By the time he'd worked his way through the crowd to talk to Anna, he was positive Trudy Lynn wasn't in the building. Widget was raising the roof in the back room.

He greeted the teen with a smile. "Hi. Boss lady gone?"

"Yup."

"You wouldn't happen to know where I'd find her, would you?"

"No. Sorry."

Cody leaned closer. "Want to give me a hint?"

The girl giggled. "You might ask Will. He knows everything."

"Thanks. I'll do that. Where would he be?"

She whispered behind her cupped hand. "He was supposed to help Farley work on the dock this afternoon."

"Got it. Thanks."

When he ducked out the door he noticed a few reporters gathering like turkey vultures circling fresh roadkill. Little wonder Trudy Lynn had felt the need to make herself scarce. If she'd given him any choice besides going by water, he'd have gladly joined her.

The Spring River was nothing like the Tuolumne, he

reasoned, hoping to come to grips with his uneasiness. He'd never been hesitant to grab a boat and try to navigate any watercourse, no matter how dangerous, so what was stopping him now? What, indeed?

It wasn't fear. Not the way he'd felt it before. Only a fool would deny being afraid during a whitewater trip. That was what heightened the excitement, made the adrenaline flow. It was a familiar part of the exhilaration.

These current emotions were different. Unlike anything else he'd experienced. It was as if he loathed the water so much he didn't even want to look at it, let alone trust himself to enter it. Where before he'd seen beauty and power, he now saw ugliness and malice. His injured knee wasn't the only thing keeping him on dry land, was it? Part of his heart and soul had also died when his client had drowned so tragically, so needlessly.

Cody was grim from retrospection when he reached the dock where Will and Farley were nailing down replacement planks. He waited on shore till one of the men looked up.

"Anna sent me to see you, Will."

"Come on out, son."

"That's okay. Looks like you're almost done. I don't mind waiting."

The old man rose stiffly to his feet. "I see my cane worked for ya."

"Very well, thanks. It's been a pleasure to get rid of those crutches."

"Glad to help." Will walked closer, inspecting their work, board by board, as he came. "So, what can I do

for ya this time? You ready to paddle your own canoe?"
He cackled at the stale joke.

"No. Thanks anyway. I can't seem to find your boss.
Anna told me you might know where she's hiding."

"I might."

"Well?"

"Miz Brown told me not to say." Drawing his fingers
and thumb slowly down his cheeks to meet at the point
of his chin, Will looked Cody up and down. "She didn't
want no reporters buggin' her. But since she asked you
to go along, I reckon it'd be okay to tell ya."

Icy needles of fear prickled along Cody's nerves.
"She didn't take a canoe?"

"She sure did. 'Bout ten minutes ago. Say, you okay,
son? You look kinda pale."

"I'm fine," Cody lied. His heart was pounding, his
mouth so dry he could hardly swallow, let alone sound
casual when he spoke. "Did she go alone?"

"Yep. I tried to talk her out of it but she's one stubborn lady. There's not a lot of traffic on the river this late
in the day, especially not till the time changes to daylight
saving next month. She promised me she'd go ashore
and call for the van before dark."

Concerned, Cody shaded his eyes and squinted at the
setting sun. "How long does she have?"

"An hour and a half. Maybe two. Depends on the lay
of the land."

Something inside Cody kept insisting he had to act,
even though the thought almost made him gag. He pointed
to an empty canoe. "How hard is it to man one of those?"

"Not hard at all," Will said. "It might be a little tough to balance or kneel to paddle with that stiff leg of yours but I wouldn't worry. Compared to them rapids you're used to, this river's easy as pie. Want me to set you up?"

"Yes," Cody said. He gritted his teeth. "Give me the works, life vest and all. If I turn the thing over I don't want to have to try to tread water."

"Might do you good," the old man offered. "I hear swimmin' is good fer bad joints."

"In warm water," Cody replied. "Trudy Lynn told me this comes from an underground spring about thirty miles north. She says it's so cold when it hits the surface they built a trout hatchery at the headwaters."

"True enough. Them trout love it. The colder the water the better."

"I'll take your word for it," Cody said flatly.

Shrugging into the bright orange life vest he slipped a map of the river into his pocket, then cautiously climbed into the waiting canoe while Farley and Will steadied it. Thankfully, there was enough room to stretch his sore leg as far as he needed for comfort.

"Okay. I'm in," he said. "I've been to all the landings with Trudy so I know what they look like. I'll catch up to her unless it gets too dark to see."

Will handed him the cane. "Better take this, too. Some of that country's pretty rugged."

"Yeah, I know." Cody gritted his teeth and steeled himself for what he was about to do. "Push me off," he said hoarsely. "I'm ready."

ELEVEN

Peace flowed over Trudy Lynn like the ripples bathing the smooth rocks beneath her canoe. She dangled her fingertips in the water and drifted with the slow current. Few course corrections were necessary in this deeper portion of the river. Water levels were holding higher than normal since the heavy rain they'd had the day Jim had disappeared, and she skimmed along above submerged hazards she'd have had to paddle around in drier times.

A red squirrel on the east bank realized he had company and scampered up the closest oak. Watching him, Trudy Lynn noticed dozens of robins. Spring was here all right. Soon, the flock would pair off and the migrating purple martins would arrive. The meadowlarks would begin their morning serenades and the steady calls of the whip-poor-will would lull her to sleep every night.

She sighed. Too bad *her* life wasn't that simple. Just when she thought she had it all figured out, along came another problem. A vivid image of Cody Keringhoven popped into her mind. *Speaking of problems.*

One quick assessment of the river told her it would be safe to close her eyes for a moment of prayer. Where should she begin? What should she ask? If she knew *that,* she'd have the dilemma half-solved.

Finally, she whispered, "Father, thank you for all this. For letting me live here." Gratitude filled her heart to overflowing. "This is a beautiful place and I am grateful for everything. I just need help dealing with the people."

Boy, was that the truth. Give her birds and squirrels and Widget and she'd be totally content, she told herself. Was that true? Was she really happy single? She'd certainly thought so until very recently. Until she'd been given the chance to spend time with Cody. Was the Lord using him to try to tell her she was on the wrong track?

Trudy Lynn's eyes popped open. She blinked in the brightness. *Whoa.* Cody might be someone's idea of the perfect husband but he certainly wasn't hers. For one thing, he was way too opinionated. Too bossy. Then again, maybe God merely wanted her to open her mind to the possibility of marriage. Even Adam had needed his Eve. It would be comforting to have someone to share both her good times and her burdens. Yeah. Like now.

Her worried musings turned to her cousin. How could Jim have vanished so completely? Finding a life vest and damaged paddle was worrisome enough. Losing a full-size canoe was nearly impossible. Even if it had floated further than normal due to the flooding, it would run aground eventually. Her camp ID and logo were stenciled on it. It should have turned up by now and so should Jim.

Lost in a fog of contradictory thoughts, Trudy Lynn

had quit paying much attention to the passing scene. A cloud of aggravating gnats buzzed around her head. A hungry one landed on her forearm.

"Ouch!" She swatted and missed. The tiny insect's escape route took it up and away, to her left. Waving her hands to disperse the swirling mass of insects she caught a flash of unusual color in her peripheral vision.

Seconds passed before she reacted. Her head snapped around. Eyes wide, she scanned the bank. Nothing seemed amiss. Still, if she let herself continue to drift on by, she'd always wonder if she should have stopped to take a better look.

Grabbing her paddle, Trudy Lynn dropped the blade into the water and used its drag like a rudder to swing the bow of the canoe toward shore. Rather than fight against the current, she'd hit the beach and hike back. It wouldn't take long. All she wanted to do was assure herself that what she'd glimpsed was unimportant. Chances were good it was nothing but a pile of trash a group of campers or picnickers had left behind.

She was ashore before she realized what a poor choice the rocky, wooded terrain was for socializing. Flying insects would be enough to discourage most tourists, and the bugs hiding on the forest floor, more than ready to dine on man or beast, would deter the diehards.

Removing her life vest and leaving it behind so it wouldn't catch on the undergrowth and slow her down, she headed into the forest. The sooner she satisfied her curiosity and got back on the river where she belonged, the happier she'd be.

* * *

Cody easily mastered maneuvers with the paddle. Now that he was committed, his misgivings were lessening. If he'd had any choice he still wouldn't have wanted to go canoeing, yet he did seem to be coping pretty well. That was a relief, given his earlier uneasiness.

Trudy Lynn hadn't exaggerated when she'd claimed it was peaceful on the Spring River. After the Tuolumne, this trip would have seemed almost boring if he hadn't been on a mission. Catching up to Trudy was the most important quest Cody had undertaken in ages. If he'd had any inkling that his hardheaded landlady was going to wander off alone, he'd have forced himself to accompany her no matter how disconcerted he'd felt. If anything bad happened...

He paddled faster. Muscles that had once piloted him through raging rapids and over foaming cataracts adopted a familiar rhythm. Cody likened himself to a marathon runner who was so focused on reaching a goal he refused to acknowledge fatigue. Good thing, too. Judging by the rosy glow in the west he was running out of time.

Brambles caught in Trudy Lynn's T-shirt and scratched her bare legs, making her wish she'd worn jeans instead of walking shorts. She could tell how high the river had most recently crested by noting the undulating piles of dead leaves and twigs it had deposited along the upper banks. No wonder poor Jim had lost some of his equipment. He must have been caught in a fearsome torrent.

One foot slipped in the slick mud, dropping her to her knees. She righted herself and grabbed a deadfall for balance. Leaving her canoe had been a mistake. Here she was, in the middle of nowhere, covered with gummy, red mud, rotting leaves and disgusting slime, chasing figments of her imagination that had probably never existed in the first place. If she hurt herself, no telling how long it would be before rescuers found her.

"I should turn back and forget it," she muttered. That was excellent advice. Unfortunately, a contrary part of her character refused to be deterred by logic. It couldn't be much farther to the place where she'd seen the flash of color. As soon as she was satisfied it was nothing, she'd gladly make for the nearest landing and phone Will to come get her.

The vegetation grew thicker, harder to traverse. A stand of young hickory trees was almost impenetrable. Trudy Lynn was about to call it quits when she spied another bright spot of paint. It was red, as she'd thought, but it wasn't trash. Even without seeing a number or name, she knew. It was one of her canoes. And the only one unaccounted for was the one Jim had taken the day he'd disappeared.

It took Trudy Lynn several more minutes to fight her way to her goal. Flood or no flood, it was clear the canoe hadn't wound up that far out of the water by accident. Though it may have floated in this direction while unmanned, it hadn't pulled itself up the bank and covered its own hull with loose brush for camouflage.

Uneasy, she stopped and peered into the surrounding woods. Shadows had deepened while she'd been on foot. Details were dimmer. Not only was the sun obviously setting, nearby trees were so close together they blocked out the usual patterns of dappled, filtered light on the leaf-strewn ground.

An unexplained tingle skittered up her spine. The fine hairs on the back of her neck tickled. She wrapped her arms around her torso and shivered, head to toe, before finding enough willpower to reclaim her self-control.

Being afraid was ridiculous. These woods were her home, her solace, her place to hide when the outside world began to close in.

Dwelling on that truth, she managed to relax a bit, though she couldn't totally banish the innate urge to chatter whether there was anyone else present or not.

"What I do next is critical," she told herself, calmed by the sound of her own voice. "I have to tag a tree next to the water so I can locate this place again when I bring the police. And I need to back out of this thicket so I don't disturb the ground any more than I already have."

Such sensible planning triggered a smile. At last she had a plausible excuse for reading all those mystery stories Will kept teasing her about. Hopefully, she'd learned enough from them to do her—and the police—some good.

She took several steps backward, then halted. "What if poor Jim is in the canoe? He could be hurt. Or worse."

If she crept closer to peek, she'd know for sure. If she

didn't let curiosity get the better of her, however, any footprints or other clues to his disappearance would be preserved. Which choice made the most sense?

Trudy Lynn had encountered dead animals in the woods a few times. Their stench was unforgettable. The air she was currently breathing was clear, fresh, unsullied, proving there were no dead bodies close by. And since no one who was incapacitated could have buried the canoe that well with himself still inside, she was reassured.

Satisfied, she gave in to the growing urge to turn and flee. Since her hands, knees and shoes were already covered with mud she took no pains to proceed slowly and avoid getting dirtier. Her impulsiveness led to a slipping, sliding descent to the river, punctuated by an occasional "Oof," or "Ugh."

She'd almost reached her beached canoe when a guttural, angry-sounding "Stop!" stood her hair on end.

She froze. Whirled. Stared, openmouthed. The man crouched on the low bluff directly above her was terrifying! He had wild, stringy hair and a beard in the same condition. His shadowed figure conveyed so much malice it took away what little breath she had left. In his hand was a rifle or shotgun, she couldn't tell which, and his clothing looked as if he'd put it on years ago and hadn't taken it off since.

"You're trespassing!" he roared. "Who are you? What are you doing here?"

Trudy Lynn hoped the good Lord would forgive her for telling a bold-faced lie because this seemed like a very dangerous moment to admit the truth. "I got lost," she called back. "Don't worry. I'm leaving."

Instead of the chastising she'd expected, the man gave a bearlike bellow and charged!

Trudy Lynn didn't know she was screaming till she heard the piercing wails and realized they had to be coming from her! She planted both hands on the prow of the canoe and shoved it into the river as far as she could wade, then gave one last mighty push and heaved herself aboard.

Instead of continuing forward, the canoe came to an abrupt halt and began rocking. Violently. She knew what she'd see before she looked back. Her pursuer had her! And he was starting to reel her in like a helpless fish.

Her paddle lay on the floor beneath her. She grabbed it and flailed wildly at him. The edge of the blade cracked against the metal rim of the canoe. With a maniacal laugh the man yanked the splintered weapon out of her hands and turned it on her.

Trudy Lynn ducked, stumbled, backpedaled. She had only a split second in which to decide. If she dived over the side she might have a better chance of survival. Staying in the canoe like a sitting duck was out of the question. There was no telling what her attacker might do if—when—he got his filthy hands on her.

I knew I should have polished up my swimming skills. Well, it was too late for regrets. From here on she'd have to either wade, swim as best she could or drown. Given this man's aura of rage and menace, any of those choices would be preferable to letting him get close enough to touch her.

* * *

A woman's screams echoed up the river and across the hills, confusing the direction the sound was coming from. Cody strained to listen. He had no idea if Trudy Lynn was the one yelling. He didn't care. Anyone that scared needed help. Fast. Hopefully, he was close enough to give it.

He plied the paddle skillfully and sent the canoe skimming along, faster and faster. In the distance, a male voice was shouting curses. Something crashed. Splintered. Banged. It sounded like a dozen men were brawling just around the next bend in the river. He had to be getting close.

The woman's screeching suddenly ceased. Cody's heart leaped, bringing the bitter taste of gall to his throat. Silence was a bad sign. It meant the situation had changed, probably not for the better.

Slewing around a curve he spotted another canoe. A man was standing in the water next to it, hip deep. Perhaps he was trying to rescue someone. That would explain the shouting.

Cody continued his rapid approach. He saw the man climb into the canoe and kneel to use his hands as oars. Sighting along a line to where the other boat was headed, Cody saw a figure splashing in the water.

He was farther away but his pace was much faster. Chances were good he'd reach the swimmer first. Elated, he shouted, "Hang on. I'm coming!"

When the person in the water screamed, "Cody!" then went under, his gut tied in a knot. He'd found Trudy Lynn.

* * *

If this is what it's like to die I don't like it. Where are the bright lights? The comforting feelings?

Trudy Lynn's toes touched bottom. Instinct spurred her to bend her knees enough for a powerful jump.

She popped to the surface, gasping and spitting. Had she really seen Cody a moment ago? Or was hallucinating an element of death by drowning?

Wet hair plastered to her face and hampered her vision. She managed another "Cody?" and a few wild strokes with her arms before going under again. This time, however, she'd grabbed a gulp of air and knew what to do.

Using the uneven riverbed as a springboard she bobbed up and down like a fish on a Pogo stick. Current kept pushing her along, yet every time she surfaced, both canoes were definitely closer. To her great relief, the one coming at her from the bank wasn't moving nearly as swiftly as the one from upriver—the one she hoped and prayed Cody was in.

It took three more bounces and a mouthful of water before Trudy Lynn was certain. It *was* Cody! She'd never been so glad to see anybody in her whole life. She didn't care if he had refused to come with her in the first place. He was here now, when it counted.

Suddenly, it occurred to her that she wasn't the only one in danger. She and Cody both were. Her attacker had dropped his gun on shore when he'd grabbed her canoe but that didn't mean he wasn't armed with a knife or something equally deadly. Plus, he was built like a grizzly bear and had an even nastier disposition. The chance of Cody being able to pull her on board with him and facilitate an escape before they were attacked was slim. Very slim. He wouldn't even try to get away because he didn't have a clue how much trouble they were in.

"Look out!" she screeched.

Down she went, this time without a full breath. It seemed like hours before she returned to the surface. Between racking coughs she hollered, "Bad!" and gestured wildly at the slower canoe.

Had Cody understood? Dog-paddling she tossed her head to flip her dripping hair away from her eyes and blinked rapidly to clear her vision. It was no use. She couldn't see his face well enough to judge.

The constant, simple prayer, *God, help us,* kept running through her mind. Even if she'd been able to come up with a more spiritual-sounding plea, this was clearly not the time for fancy words. They were in deep trouble. Getting out of it was going to take more than mere physical ability. If any situation in her life had ever needed divine intervention, this was it.

Cody was confused. Will had been certain his boss had set out alone. So who was the other rescuer? What had happened to Trudy Lynn's canoe? And why had she removed her life vest and gone into the water when she knew she was a poor swimmer? None of it made sense, especially not the guy trying to row after her using nothing but his bare hands.

"It's okay. I'll get her," Cody called.

He wouldn't have taken his eyes off Trudy Lynn for an instant if the other man hadn't cursed in reply. He chanced a swift glance. The malice reflected in the dark glare that met his was all the clarification Cody needed. Whatever the guy's motive was for going after Trudy Lynn, it sure wasn't benevolent.

The scenario took on a totally different connotation. Cody stiffened, wary. Getting Trudy Lynn out of the water and into his canoe should be pretty easy. Doing that while facing opposition promised to be trickier.

He'd planned to steer to her right, positioning himself so the other canoe could assist. Now, his plans changed.

He turned the blade of his paddle to add drag at the last second, altered course to put himself between Trudy and the other man and reached for her. One of her hands was all that wasn't submerged. Grabbing it and hanging on, he pulled her over the side so she hung beside him, head down in the boat, feet still in the water.

"Breathe!" he ordered. "Breathe."

The sweetest sound he'd ever heard was her gagging, hacking cough. "That's it, honey. Don't fight it. Get it all out."

She raised her head slightly and tried unsuccessfully to speak.

Cody thumped her between her shoulder blades. "I know. He's bad news. I figured that out." The other canoe was nearing. "I'll take care of it."

Her faint "Be careful" warmed his heart.

"I will. Hang on. I'm going to pull you the rest of the way in just in case things get rough."

To his delight and further relief, Trudy Lynn had regained enough strength to help him. Though she still sounded as if she was trying to imitate Sailor's barking, she sat up as soon as she was fully aboard.

Her eyes were red and wild-looking. Her hair was streaming river water. Her arms and calves were covered with welts and scratches. Cody's heart rejoiced. He had never been so glad to see her.

There were only a few seconds left before the other canoe would pull alongside. Cupping her cheeks, he drew her closer and placed a light kiss on her forehead.

Tears filled Trudy Lynn's eyes and slid, unnoticed, down her already wet face. She was so relieved, so thankful, she just wanted to throw herself into Cody's arms, cling to him and sob. A shred of sensibility held her back. Cody was already at a physical disadvantage. Adding emotion to the mix and distracting him from the danger, even for an instant, would be idiotic.

Cody swiveled his torso and faced his foe. "We're fine. Everything's under control. You can go."

"I ain't goin' nowhere. I'll take care of both of you if I have to," came the gravelly reply.

Nothing about the man's threat struck Trudy Lynn as a show of false bravado. She could tell that Cody agreed, because his fists were clenched and he was clearly bracing for an attack. If the two men had been standing, toe-to-toe, Cody's injured knee would have been a significant negative factor. Seated, however, they were more evenly matched.

"Oh, please, God," she whispered prayerfully.

Cody didn't look a bit worried, certainly not as frazzled as she felt.

"I don't see the problem here," Cody told the man evenly. "Suppose I take the lady on down the river with me? Would that satisfy you?"

"Humph." He let out a string of curses. "Don't suppose it would. She was trespassin' on my land."

"In that case, we apologize. If there was any damage done we'll be happy to make restitution. Just contact the Spring River Camp or send a bill. You know where that's located, don't you."

"Oh, yeah," the swarthy man drawled. "I surely do."

Trudy Lynn laid her hand on Cody's arm to get his attention and felt his skin twitch beneath her touch. "Don't tell him any more."

He cast a sidelong glance in her general direction while continuing to focus most of his attention on their accuser. "Why not? It's no secret. All he has to do is look at the names printed on your canoes."

"I know, but…" She cupped her hand around her mouth and leaned closer to whisper, "I found the one Jim took. Somebody tried to bury it. It's right over there."

Although she didn't actually point, Trudy Lynn did stare at the thicket where she'd uncovered the missing canoe. Too late, she realized she'd inadvertently done the very thing she'd vowed to avoid. She'd distracted Cody.

A dark blur rose up on one side of them. The other man leaped and tackled Cody squarely in the chest.

Trudy Lynn shouted, "Look out!" but her warning

came too late. Momentum carried both men over the side with a sickening splash.

Stunned, she watched them sink. Together.

TWELVE

The shock of hitting the water wasn't incapacitating. The vivid recollection of the last time he'd been catapulted into an icy river was. Cody didn't feel pain, only sorrow and deep regret. His brain tried to shelter him by shutting off all thought while his life jacket gave him the buoyancy to rise to the surface without trying.

The pressure of strong hands grasping his throat snapped him back to reality. He slipped both hands between his opponent's arms and shoved upward, breaking the vicelike grip.

Instead of immediately resuming his efforts to strangle Cody, the man clutched at his life vest and tore it away, then grabbed him again and pulled him under.

Cody kicked and tore at his opponent, oblivious to anything but the danger to Trudy Lynn. He didn't even want to think about what might happen to her if he was defeated.

Freeing himself once again, he struck out for the surface. For life-giving air. As soon as his head was out of the water he rejoiced. Trudy Lynn was still safe in his canoe. What a relief!

He gulped down a quick breath and shouted," Stay back!" while he waited for his attacker to pop up nearby.

Something grabbed his ankle instead. Pulled him under. Kept him there till he thought his lungs would burst. It was impossible to throw a forceful punch through water. If this fight came to a contest of brute strength, Cody wasn't positive he'd win. He wasn't filled with brilliant ideas for outsmarting his opponent, either.

The top of his head banged against a hull, making a hollow thud. The attacker's empty boat must be directly above them. He didn't know exactly how canoes behaved when inverted but he could guess. Large inflatable rafts were hard to get out from under, especially in a swift current, and this stretch of the river was gaining speed. If he could turn the canoe over unexpectedly, maybe that would give him an advantage. It was worth a try. At this point, anything was.

Cody lunged. Twisted into position. Set his feet. Using his opponent as a springboard he managed to thrust one arm out of the water far enough to grab the side rim of the empty canoe. If the other man continued to try to drag him down, the combined mass of Cody and the canoe should provide the necessary counterbalance.

It did. Cody would have cheered if he hadn't been submerged. Experience told him a small pocket of air was waiting beneath the overturned hull. Gasping, he bobbed into the empty space and filled his aching lungs while his confused enemy swam away. The question was, which way had the guy gone? Toward Trudy Lynn?

Frustrated with himself for being unsure, Cody took

one last gulping breath before ducking out from under the inverted hull. As his head broke the surface he swiveled. His heart stopped. "No!"

The attacker had grabbed onto the side of the canoe Trudy Lynn occupied and was working his way toward her, hand over hand.

"The paddle!" Cody shouted. "Use the paddle!"

"No! I won't leave you." She dodged the grasping fingers that kept clawing at her.

"Not to *row* with," Cody bellowed. "Hit him!"

Trudy Lynn didn't have to be told twice. Loving her neighbor had ended the minute said neighbor had tried to drown Cody.

The oar shaft fit her fists like a baseball bat. She wasn't going to make the mistake of swinging at the man's hands and breaking this paddle the way she had the other one. No, sir. She was going to do what she had to do.

Thoughts of personal accountability made her hesitate for an instant. Was it really right to bash him? What if she *killed* him?

"Leave us alone," she shouted shrilly. "Just leave us alone. We weren't hurting you."

The man's laugh was abrasive. "You are dumber than dirt, aren't you?" He wiggled his fingers. "C'mon. Give me that thing. Hand it over. Or else."

While she and the swarthy man had been arguing, Cody had swum into reach. Trudy Lynn's wide-eyed gaze touched on him. Too late, she realized her carelessness had cost him the element of surprise.

The attacker's eyes narrowed. Looking over his shoulder he grinned with malevolence. "I thought I was rid of you. Guess I'm gonna have to whup you some more."

Trudy Lynn could see pain in Cody's eyes. There was no telling how badly this encounter had affected his injured leg. Well, she wasn't going to just sit there and let him be hurt anymore.

The man let go of the canoe and made a lunge for Cody's throat.

That did it. Trudy Lynn drew back and swung. The horrible noise of the broadside to the man's head echoed in her ears and lingered in her conscience. It had sounded for all the world like a ripe watermelon being dropped onto a hard surface!

Cody lifted his foe's face out of the water.

"Did I kill him?" Trudy Lynn asked breathlessly. "I didn't mean to hit him so hard. Honest, I didn't."

"He's not dead, just groggy," Cody answered. "He'll probably have a headache, though. Help me get him out of the water. Then we'll call the sheriff. This time, we have proof."

Trudy Lynn peered into lengthening shadows along the shore. "Not exactly. We've drifted way past the place where I found Jim's canoe. I'm pretty sure I can locate it again if we start upstream and float down in the daylight, but it's way too late to go back and try it, now."

"Okay." Cody rolled the man's limp body onto its back and hooked one arm under the bearded chin. Held that way, his burden floated safely and with little effort. "Think you can tow us in like this?"

"Sure. After the day I've had I can do anything."

"I'll settle for hitching a ride to shore and finding the quickest way out of this jungle," Cody said. "I don't know about you, but I'm beat."

Trudy Lynn's heart swelled with pride in her rescuer. "You were wonderful. I don't know what I'd have done if you hadn't come along when you did."

"I don't even want to think about it."

"I do," she replied. "I'll never forget today. I have no doubt you saved my life. If there's ever anything I can do to pay you back, just let me know. No matter what it is or how much it costs. All you have to do is say the word and I'll do whatever I can. I promise."

"Good. Then how about you stop talking and start rowing. Our friend is beginning to wiggle. The sooner we get him tied up so he can't cause any more trouble, the happier I'll be."

"I'm pretty happy already." Trudy Lynn grinned. Plying the paddle skillfully, she rowed them toward shore at an angle, using the current to assist.

"You should be happy," Cody said. "Looks like we're finally going to get some answers about your cousin."

"Oh, that. Right." A rush of embarrassment colored her cheeks. They'd reached the shallows where Cody was able to stand. Vaulting over the side of the boat into the waist-deep water, Trudy Lynn helped him haul his semi-conscious burden onto dry land.

"We'd better hurry. He's waking up," Cody said.

"Grab the mooring rope off the canoe. We'll tie him to a tree till the sheriff gets here."

Her head snapped around. "Oops. Looks like I'm going to have to get wet again."

"You let it drift? I don't believe this."

"Don't get excited, okay? I didn't take time to beach it because I was in a hurry to help you. It's no big deal. I'll get it back." She was already moving that direction.

"You can't swim well, remember?"

The gruffness of his voice rankled her. "I'm not likely to forget. I'm just going to wade out a little way."

"No. You stay here. I'll go."

"Don't be silly. I do this kind of thing all the time."

Trudy Lynn quickly retrieved the canoe, dragged it up the bank and untied the braided nylon rope at its bow.

Jaw set, eyes narrowed, Cody stared at her. "You don't have to keep reminding me you're more capable than I am."

"What? What are you talking about?"

"Chasing that loose canoe. I may not be as fast on my feet as you are but I could have caught it."

"I know that."

"You don't act like you do."

Trudy Lynn rolled her eyes to emphasize how silly she thought he was. "You were busy. I certainly didn't want to trade places with you and have our friend wake up while you were gone. I chase loose boats all the time. If I'd waited till we were done arguing about who should go, the stupid canoe could have drifted out of everybody's reach. *Then* where would we be? On foot, that's where."

She thrust the coil of rope at him. "Here. Do you want this or don't you?"

Cody's initial hesitation and the begrudging way he finally accepted the rope told her he wasn't convinced she'd meant no disrespect. Well, too bad. He was going to have to get used to the way she took charge when something needed to be done. She wasn't about to sit back and act like a helpless female in need of coddling. Her mother had been that kind of woman and look what had happened.

Thinking of her father's kindness reminded her of how much she'd sensed the same tender concern from Cody. He cared. That was why he'd snapped at her for going into the river again.

Approaching as soon as he'd finished trussing their captive to a tree, Trudy Lynn placed her hand on his forearm in a show of conciliation. "I'm sorry. You were right. It was stupid of me not to stop and put on a life vest."

His astonished reaction made her giggle. "Hey, don't look so surprised. I do occasionally make mistakes. There just wasn't time to explain. Your canoe was about to break out into the faster current and…"

"I know that," Cody said. "I shouldn't have jumped to conclusions. I'm sorry, too." A half smile began to lift the corner of his mouth. "So, are you done scaring me to death?"

"I hope so."

"Good. Then let's call the sheriff. My cell phone's so full of water it gurgles. Do you have a dry one?"

"No. My pack was in the canoe that turned over."

"Terrific. How far is it to the next landing?"

"Less than a mile." Eyeing their captive she noticed he was beginning to struggle against his bonds. "Will it be safe to leave him for a little while?"

"He won't get away," Cody said flatly.

"I'm more worried about his head. He acts like he's okay but I conked him awfully hard."

"The sooner we get to a phone and call, the sooner he can be checked out by a doctor. Come on. Let's go."

Trudy Lynn paused and stopped him with a gentle touch. "Wait. I want to thank you."

"You already did."

"I mean properly."

Standing on tiptoe, she slipped her hands around his neck, tilted her head back and felt his warm breath on her face. Ever since he'd hauled her out of the river and kissed her on the forehead she'd wanted to do this. There might never be a better time than right now.

"I was coughing so much you got it all wrong." She smiled as she pointed to her lips. "It goes right here."

"What does?"

There was no question he was teasing. The sparkle in his azure eyes confirmed it. "This," she said, an instant before she kissed him gently, briefly. "Thank you for saving my life."

The ambulance got lost on unmarked dirt roads so the sheriff loaded the injured man into his car and personally delivered him to the hospital.

Trudy Lynn had called Will from the landing and told

him to bring the truck with the overhead rack to haul the canoes home. She and Cody had instructions to report to the sheriff's office as soon as possible.

Wedged into the front seat of the pickup between Will and Cody, she shivered. "I may never get warm again."

Cody's arm had been draped across the back of the seat. He lowered it and patted her opposite shoulder. "It's probably shock more than temperature that's making you feel cold. Maybe we'd better take you to the emergency room for a checkup, too."

"Oh, no. That's where the sheriff took that man. I'm not going anywhere near him."

To her left, Will chuckled. "Scared ya good, did he?"

"You could say that."

She gazed up at Cody, supremely grateful for his strength and levelheadedness in the recent crisis. "I'm thankful we both survived. I had my doubts for a while there, especially when that canoe flipped over on top of you. It never dawned on me you'd done it on purpose."

"I was kind of short of options." His hold tightened just enough to let her know his arm was still around her. "I'd have preferred working in a faster current. I'm more used to handling myself in that kind of situation."

"I think you did just fine," she said.

"So did you. That's quite a swing you have."

She grimaced. "Don't remind me. I feel awful about it."

"You shouldn't."

"Yes, I should. I'm supposed to trust the Lord to take care of me."

Cody's rich laughter rose above Will's accompanying chuckle.

Trudy Lynn scowled. "Okay, you two. What's so funny?"

"You are," Cody said. "I can't help thinking of how handy that paddle was when you needed it. I doubt God expects us to sit back and act like helpless victims, especially not when He's provided a means of self-defense."

"Right," the older man said. "The Good Book's full of teachin' like that." He cackled. "'Course, it's also possible He was usin' *you* to take care of our girl."

Trudy Lynn let centrifugal force slue her against Cody as the truck rounded a corner, then stayed close to him by choice. "I have to agree," she said, nodding. "If you hadn't pulled me out of the river when you did, I wouldn't have been alive to swing a paddle."

She saw his eyes close briefly before he sighed and said, "I know."

There was so much poignancy and heartfelt relief in his voice she almost wept.

"I may have seen the man before," Trudy Lynn told the sheriff a little later, "but I can't place him. The important thing is, I found Jim's canoe."

"So you say. Are you sure?"

"Positive."

"You saw the name and number on it, then?"

"Well, no, but..." She looked to Cody for moral support. There was rancor and disbelief in the way he was staring at the lawman.

"If Ms. Brown says she found one of her canoes, she found one. Period," Cody said firmly. "What're you going to do about it?"

The portly sheriff shrugged. "Tonight? Nothing. Buford swears that boat is his and he caught you two trespassing. They're keepin' him in the hospital at least till tomorrow. For observation, they said. That's some knot on the head you gave him. You'll be lucky if Buford don't press charges."

"Press charges for self-defense?" Cody was scowling.

"Your word against his. He is the one landed in the emergency room."

"For good reason," Cody argued.

"Maybe. No sense gettin' carried away. A little neighborly kindness might settle the whole thing."

Cody got to his feet. "We'll see what the state police have to say about that." He looked to Trudy Lynn. "Come on. Let's go before I say something I'll be sorry for."

"Good luck," the sheriff drawled. "Those state boys packed up their trucks and lit out while you two were beatin' up poor ol' Buford. I reckon they're all the way to Little Rock by now."

"Then we'll phone their office in the morning," Trudy Lynn said. Head high, spine stiff, she led the way out of the building. Once she and Cody were back on the street, however, she began to show fatigue and disillusionment.

"You okay?" he asked.

"Fine." She gave him a wry smile. "No, not fine. Did he just call me a liar?"

"Not exactly. But it did sound like he thinks you're a hysterical female who was imagining things."

"That's almost as bad."

"*I* believe you."

"I know you do. Thanks. That means a lot to me."

Trudy Lynn saw him start to reach for her hand, then stop himself. Little wonder. She'd probably scared him to death when she'd kissed him. What had come over her? She wasn't the kind to pass out affection carelessly so why in the world had she given in to such an irrational urge? The man must think the worst of her.

Well, why shouldn't he? she countered. *I certainly think it.*

Try as she might, Trudy Lynn couldn't come up with an acceptable rationale for the unusual way she had behaved. Thankfulness didn't cover it. Neither did being free from danger. She'd been beholden to others in the past and hadn't felt the need to throw herself into their arms as a result. What was it about Cody Keringhoven that brought out the wild side of her?

Perhaps *wild* wasn't the right term. She hadn't felt out of control. On the contrary, she'd sensed a strength of purpose, a need to reveal her emotions and see what Cody's response might be. Now that she'd seen his reaction, however, she was beginning to wish she'd kept her distance.

She sighed. "Well, what now? I suppose we should let Will take us back to camp."

"Sounds like a good idea to me." Cody used the cane

as he walked beside her toward the waiting truck. "We're both dead tired. And we need a phone."

"To call Little Rock?"

"Yes. Are you up to it or shall I do it for you?"

"Whatever." Trudy Lynn shrugged. "I'm too tired and sore to care." She paused, her hand on the door handle of the pickup. "Shame on me. Here I am, complaining over little aches and pains like a sissy when it's you I should be thinking of. How's your leg?"

"Forget it. It's okay." Cody reached to open the door for her.

"No, it's not okay."

"Yes, it is." He swung the door back and gestured as Will started the motor. "In you go."

"But you're limping."

"I always do," Cody said solemnly. "That's never going to change."

"Like the color of your eyes. They'll always be blue."

"I beg your pardon?"

Giving him a satisfied smile she scooted to the center of the bench seat to make room. "Blue eyes are part of how you're made. You're used to them because you've always had them but there's really no difference between that and your limp. It just *is*. Like being tall or short, blond or brunette—you get the idea."

"There's no comparison." Cody climbed in and slammed the door.

"Sure there is. You've been so busy thinking about what's wrong or different, you've lost sight of the stuff that's wonderful."

"Wonderful?" He tapped the tip of the cane on his shoe. "You call this wonderful? Humph. I sure don't."

"Maybe that's because you've forgotten who made you in the first place. Or who kept you out of the accident that killed your mother. Or who guided your sister to look for her birth family and reunited all of you. Or who put you in the right place at the right time to come to my rescue."

"You mean God." It wasn't a question.

"Yes, I do. Think about it. Every time you complain you dishonor your creator. You're as worthwhile in God's eyes as you were before. It's time you recognized your value as a human being and started thanking Him for sparing your life instead of griping about a little limp."

Cody stared at her. "Are you through?"

"Yes." She pulled a face and bowed her head rather than continue to make eye contact with him. "I guess so. I can't think of anything else to say."

Will guffawed when Cody said, "Now that I *am* thankful for."

THIRTEEN

Cody hadn't dozed off till nearly dawn. As long as his brain was racing, there was no way he could unwind enough to sleep.

He'd spoken to a dispatcher at the Arkansas State Police headquarters as soon as he and the others had gotten back to camp. The men who had been looking into Jim's disappearance had other duties. It seemed that Jim was no longer considered a high priority according to the local sheriff.

Cody couldn't blame them for pulling out; he just wished their orders had come through a day or two later. He flexed his knee. It hurt. That figured. The big surprise was how little its condition had changed. In spite of all the stress of the fight and subsequent short hike to the landing, he didn't feel any worse than before.

"Trudy Lynn would call that a blessing," he muttered. Well, maybe she was right. Maybe it was. At least he was still on his feet and hadn't had to go back to using crutches. That meant their next move wasn't as limited as he'd originally thought.

During the night, he'd decided they should revisit the scene of the attack as soon as possible. They needed to act before good old Buford was discharged from the hospital. Once the man was back on the street there was no telling how fast he'd be able to dispose of the canoe and any other evidence tying Jim to his property—including the young man's dead body.

Cody was about to ask for a ride up the hill to the camp store when he heard the ATV stop outside. Sailor was panting, wagging and eagerly looking at the closed door.

To Cody's delight his caller was Trudy Lynn instead of Will. "Hi! I was about to call you. I had an idea."

"Me, too."

She bent to greet Sailor with open arms and was almost bowled over by his exuberance. Ruffling his silky ears she smiled at Cody. "I found out more about Buford. Will says the guy owns hundreds of acres of forest land that he's never done anything with. Everybody assumed he was saving it for hunting, especially after he painted the perimeter trees with that lavender-colored paint they use for posting, and stuck up No Hunting signs on every corner. Most of the land is inaccessible except by water, which is why the ambulance had so much trouble finding their way."

"I wonder how the sheriff managed."

"He's an old-timer. Been here all his life. Will says Buford and the sheriff used to go fishing and hunting together when they were young. I imagine that's how he learned his way around."

"Interesting."

"I thought so." Trudy Lynn straightened. "I'm not saying the sheriff is crooked or anything. I doubt he is. But in view of that personal connection I think it might be wise to try to locate Jim's canoe again. Maybe take a few pictures. Our new buddy is still in the hospital. I checked. I'm heading downriver right now. Want to come along?"

Cody chuckled softly. "Gladly. They say great minds think alike. That's exactly what I was about to suggest."

"You're not going to beg off this time?"

"Not a chance, lady." Coming down the steps with the help of the hand-carved cane, he paused. "If I thought I could find that canoe by myself I'd leave you behind. Since that's probably impossible, I'm going to stick to you like glue. Buford may have friends we don't know about. I'm not letting you go out there alone."

"You think I can't take care of myself?"

"I know you can't. Remember?"

"How could I forget? You keep reminding me."

"I'll stop mentioning it as soon as you quit acting like you still think you're invincible," Cody said soberly. "I used to believe I was the best, that the Tuolumne couldn't touch me because I knew it so well. I was wrong. I was no more in charge in that situation than you are in this one."

"I know." Trudy Lynn reached to gently pat his cheek. "The difference is, I don't see my life as a series of random events. I may not have control in the way you meant but I trust God to bring me through. Somehow." She began to smile crookedly. "That said, I'd still swing an oar again if I felt I had to."

He stood, gazed into her eyes for a long moment, then nodded. "Good. Let me shut Sailor in the cabin and I'll be ready. The sooner we get going, the sooner we'll have the proof we need."

"Did you bring a camera?" Cody asked as they floated with the current, rowing mostly to guide their canoe into the deepest parts of the channel.

"In my jacket pocket." Trudy Lynn's nerves were definitely on edge. "We're getting close."

"Which side?"

"The left," she said. "I think it was… There! Over there. See it?"

"No." He shaded his eyes and squinted. "Where?"

"That way." She pointed. "A spot of red. In the bushes. It's only visible for a second in passing. I can't believe I saw it the first time."

"Neither can I." Cody worked with her as she expertly maneuvered their craft out of the main channel and into quieter water.

"This is it. The place I went ashore!" She vaulted over the side into hip-deep water and started to tow the canoe toward the bank.

"Slow down. Take your time. If the evidence is still there you don't have to strain."

"I want to! Don't you see? This vindicates me. I'm not imagining things and I'm not hysterical. The sheriff will have to believe me now. You'll see the canoe for yourself. And we'll have pictures, too."

"Okay." Cody nodded reluctantly. "Hold this thing

steady while I get out, will you? I don't mind wet feet but I'd prefer to keep my clothes relatively dry. This time."

"I thought you weren't going to remind me anymore."

"Wrong." Cody swung his good leg out of the canoe first. "I said I'd stop when you began to act sensibly." One eyebrow arched as a lopsided smirk lifted the corners of his mouth. "That hasn't happened yet."

"It has so." Tugging the canoe up on the sandy bank, Trudy Lynn secured it to a hickory sapling with the mooring rope. "There. See? Safe and sensible. Can I take my life jacket off now or do I have to keep it on to satisfy your overblown ideas of proper precautions?"

"You can take it off," Cody said dryly. "Just don't go charging back into the water without it."

She saluted with mock sincerity. "Yes, sir, captain, sir. Whatever you say." Clearly, her companion was not amused. Well, too bad. She'd suffered enough. Having one less unknown to cope with was going to be a real relief. And maybe, just maybe, something in or near the canoe would lead them to clues about Jim's whereabouts.

"It's this way," she said, taking the lead. "Watch yourself. Some of those sticker vines are killers. I must have tripped a dozen times when I was here before."

"Is that where you got all those scratches?"

"Most of them. It's not usually a good idea to go into a thicket, especially not once the creepy-crawlies come out for the summer. Hopefully, we're early enough in the season to miss most of them."

"Hopefully."

Cody was keeping pace. Good. She didn't want to

overtax him but she didn't want to have to slow down, either. The sooner they got the canoe uncovered and proved to themselves it truly was Jim's, the sooner she'd be rid of the churning feeling in her stomach and the throbbing in her temples.

Trudy pushed aside a clump of young cedars. "Here!" she shouted over her shoulder. "It's right here, like I said."

"Wait!"

She paused. "What for?"

"Suppose it's booby-trapped?"

"It can't be. I was already here once. Remember?"

"Yes." He stepped up beside her and spoke quietly. "But that was yesterday. Something could have changed since then. And I'd keep my voice down if I were you. Sound carries well out here. No telling who might overhear us."

"Buford's in the hospital."

"Who says he was out here alone?"

"Nobody else chased me."

"Which only means they didn't see you, not that they weren't here."

"Are you always this cynical?"

"I am when it's the wisest course to follow," Cody answered. "You're the kind of person who'd stand there and stare at the sky, looking for a flight of mallards, if somebody yelled, *duck.* I'd assume the worst and hit the dirt. If that's being cynical then I'm guilty as charged."

"I'd never thought of it quite that way."

"Well, try, at least while we're out here. Now start taking pictures. I'll stand guard."

"Okay. You're the boss. Whatever you say." She smiled. "There, does that make you happy?"

"Ecstatic." He was already scanning the surrounding woods. "Where were you when Buford jumped you?"

"Ten or fifteen yards to your left." Trudy Lynn pointed. "He came from up there on that little bluff. The one with the poison ivy all over it."

The expression on Cody's face when his head snapped around was priceless. She giggled. "Just kidding."

He looked as though he was tempted to chastise her again. Instead, he mellowed. "All right. I'll cool it, too. Just take your pictures so we can get out of here. This place gives me the creeps."

Trudy Lynn silently shared his unsettling observation. There was a threatening feel to this place. It wasn't merely because she'd found the missing canoe or because she'd been accosted nearby. It was more. There was a sense of unnamed dread in the still, humid air, an aura of menace she couldn't ignore or explain away.

At first, she'd assumed her imagination was simply working overtime. Since Cody had had the same reaction, however, she was beginning to take her inner warnings a lot more seriously.

Her skin crawled. The fine hair on the back of her neck prickled. Cody was right. The sooner they got out of there, the better.

Trudy Lynn snapped a final picture. "Okay. That's enough. Let's go."

When she turned, she found Cody three-quarters of

the way up the hill she'd teased him about. "What do you think you're doing?"

"Seeing what's up here." He paused to glance down at her. "I was curious."

"You shouldn't be doing that. Not with your sore knee."

"It's permanently attached to the rest of me. I couldn't leave it behind if I wanted to. I can make it. You coming?"

"No. I don't need to see any more. Neither do you."

"I'll be down in a sec. I'm almost to the top."

"Cody…"

"Nag, nag, nag. Has anybody ever told you that you talk too much?"

"Yes. You have. Often."

"That's because you do it so regularly."

"Flattery will get you nowhere, mister." She shivered. "I keep feeling like we're being watched."

"Maybe we are. Or were. That's one of the things I aim to find out."

She gave a nervous giggle. "You *aim* to? You've only been in Arkansas a couple of weeks and you're already starting to pick up native speech patterns. Next, you'll be saying you're *fixin'* to do something."

"I am. I'm fixin' to get to the top of this hill and have a look around as soon as you quit harassing me."

"Oh, for…" Trudy Lynn bit back the rest. "Go ahead. Wreck your leg if that's what you want. I'll be waiting in the canoe."

She saw Cody's shoulders shake with silent laughter as he resumed his climb. In seconds, he'd crested the rise and disappeared from sight.

Trudy Lynn's patience quickly wore thin. "Cody? You still there? What do you see?"

There was no answer. The forest was deathly silent, save for the hushed gurgle of the Spring River. Trudy Lynn had never felt more alone, not even when she'd been fleeing in fear for her life.

She cupped her hands around her mouth, set aside caution and called, "Cody! Answer me."

There was no reply. No sound to indicate he was even there, let alone confirm that he was all right.

Heart racing, Trudy Lynn visualized horrible catastrophes. Her breath shuddered, faltered, then resumed with urgency. Anxiety had placed a pillow of worry over her face and it was smothering her.

How could Cody do this to her? Didn't he know how frantic she'd be? Didn't he care?

Of course he cared. He'd proved that over and over. He wouldn't hide, not even to play a joke on her. Doing such a thing would be cruel and he was anything but that.

So where was he? Should she try to follow him or was it silly to fret? If he got the mistaken idea she thought he wasn't capable enough to make the climb by himself it would hurt his feelings. On the other hand, suppose he did need help and she wasn't there to offer it? Then what?

Clenching her fists and gritting her teeth she prayed simply, *Father! Help!*

No polished, perfect-sounding prayer had ever given her quicker peace. Taking a deep breath she began to regain a semblance of self-control. Everything would be fine. Cody had probably stepped away from the edge and hadn't heard her calling him, that was all. She'd go back to the canoe and wait, as promised. As soon as he was satisfied there was nothing sinister lurking at the top of the hill, he'd return. He was a big, strong guy. He didn't need her, or anybody else, to prop him up.

Speaking of propping, she thought, nearing the beached canoe, *he left the cane behind.* Maybe she should take it to him. That sounded like a plausible excuse, assuming she actually ended up needing to explain her actions. Then again, what was wrong with taking his advice and exercising a little patience?

She smiled. *Patience.* That was the key. All she had to do was ready the canoe and sit there till Cody got back. No sweat, no fuss, no problem.

Shading her eyes with her hand she was watching the last place she'd seen him when she heard someone—or something—crashing through the distant underbrush! This was no stealthy approach. It was a stampede. And the sound was getting closer. Fast!

Trudy Lynn hefted the cane and took a defensive stance, then thought better of it. She'd walked away from similar circumstances twice. There was no sense tempting the Lord and trying for a third victory when she could just as easily flee. Whatever was charging toward her could have the canoe and everything in it. But it couldn't have her. No siree. She was out of there. *Now.*

She fought her way through the knee-deep brush to the base of the incline and began to scamper higher. Brambles tore at her arms and caught in her hair. Pliable twigs snapped back and whipped against her cheeks, stinging like the horse nettle that grew wild in the meadows and along the fencerows.

Behind her, the noise had ceased, at least temporarily. Trudy Lynn wasn't about to stop long enough to sneak a peek and see if she could tell what was back there. Uh-uh. No way. She was almost to the crest. To Cody. Nothing could stop her now. Not even the unseen demons that had driven her to begin that haphazard climb.

One hand grasped at protruding tree roots while the other flattened, palm down, on a horizontal patch of soft moss. She threw herself over the top of the bank with more proficiency than she'd dreamed possible and landed with an "Oof", not twenty feet from Cody.

He was staring into the distance. He didn't do anything when she said, "Cody?", except put a finger to his lips.

"Shush."

Trudy Lynn tried to wipe the sticky red mud off her hands and knees as she clambered to her feet. The task was hopeless. "Why didn't you answer me? Huh? Do you know how worried I was?"

"Be quiet. Listen. Hear that?"

"No. I'll tell you what I *did* hear. A monster of some kind. It made enough noise for ten men. Sounded like an elephant was clomping around." She held out the cane. "I brought this along in case I needed to defend myself. Do you want it?"

"No." Scowling, Cody held up his hand. "Will you please be quiet? I thought I heard voices a minute ago.

I was trying to decide which direction they were coming from when you showed up and started jabbering."

"I was just asking a simple question. You don't have to bite my head off." The stern look he sent her reminded Trudy Lynn of a similar expression she'd seen on her father's face, especially whenever her exuberance had become too overwhelming for him.

She grimaced. "Okay, okay. I'll be quiet."

Nervousness kept her from maintaining her silence for long. "Well? Do you hear anything? I don't. I sure heard plenty before I came up here after you. I don't know what it was. It kept getting closer and closer. I…"

Cody had faced her and stepped close. Very close. He grasped her upper arms firmly. Trudy Lynn gazed up at him just as he bent to place his lips on hers.

She'd closed her eyes to savor the moment until she realized this kiss was lacking the emotional wallop of their earlier efforts.

She blinked, confused. Cody was frowning and surreptitiously watching the woods. He wasn't being romantic. He was only kissing her to shut her up!

She pushed away. "Why you…you…"

Suddenly, a faint sound reached her. Cody *had* heard someone calling out. She held her breath. "I hear it, too," she said, straining to listen. "It's coming from over that way, I think."

"Can you recognize the voice?"

"I don't know. It…it sounds like… Jim!"

"Are you sure?" Cody asked.

"Positive! He's hollering for help."

"Okay. Then we'll…"

He clamped his jaw closed. Might as well save his breath. Trudy Lynn already had taken off. The cane lay at his feet. She was tearing recklessly through the woods toward who knows what, and she was totally defenseless.

FOURTEEN

Cody grabbed the cane and started after her. "Wait! Use your head."

She slowed. Whirled. Stared at him. "I am. Come on. We have to save Jim."

"Not if it gets us into hot water."

"Don't be silly. Listen. He sounds pitiful."

"He's also the one who stole from you."

"I know. But…"

"No buts," Cody said, joining her and taking her arm to keep her from running off before he'd had his say. "If that really is Jim, his voice is loud and strong. A few more minutes won't matter. We can't just barge in on whoever's holding him and expect them to hand him over because we ask politely. We need a plan."

"You mean we need to follow *your* plan, don't you? Well, it just so happens I have a few ideas of my own."

"Fine. What are they?"

Fidgeting, Trudy Lynn chewed her lower lip. "First, I'm going to find out exactly where Jim is."

"Okay. Then what?" When she stiffened and averted her gaze Cody knew she'd been bluffing.

"Then, I'll have enough information to make a sensible decision," she said.

"Fair enough. We'll reconnoiter together." He loosened his hold on her arm. "Agreed?"

"Okay. Agreed." She gestured toward the cane. "Are you going to be able to make it?"

"Unless I have to climb trees or leap canyons." It pleased him to see her start to smile.

"I thought you were going to say, 'leap tall buildings in a single bound.'"

"I'm good, but I'm not *that* good."

"Oh, I don't know. You were pretty impressive when Buford was trying to drown me."

Cody couldn't help noticing how pink her cheeks had grown. Embarrassment confirmed her candor. Coming from someone as stubborn and hardheaded as Trudy Lynn Brown, the compliment meant a lot. When he was around her he didn't feel defective or disabled. Not anymore. She didn't baby him, yet she wasn't cruel or off-putting, either. She might not always agree with him but she always accepted him.

That conclusion gave him pause. Perhaps he'd do well to give her the same consideration.

Up ahead, Trudy Lynn paused and raised her hand, then ducked behind the broad trunk of an oak.

Cody joined her. "What do you see?"

"Some kind of building. I think that's where the calls for help are coming from."

He leaned closer to her shoulder so he could peer past. The sweet, clean fragrance of her hair was so appealing, so distracting, he paused to take a deep breath before stepping back and saying, "I think so, too. Somebody's tacked plastic to a rough framework. Looks like a makeshift greenhouse."

"Out here? There isn't any electricity. Even if they had their own well they couldn't pump water without a generator."

"Maybe they have one." Cody's senses were still on overload from being so close to Trudy Lynn. That would never do. He needed to be vigilant. Ready for anything.

"Right, maybe they do," she whispered. "What now?"

"I don't know. You're supposed to be the one with the rescue plan." If he hadn't been trying to remain secretive he'd have laughed aloud at her look of consternation. "Okay. Tell you what. Let's circle around and check everything carefully before we stumble into an ambush. You go one way and I'll go the other. When we meet on the opposite side, we'll talk. How does that sound?"

"Logical," Trudy Lynn muttered.

"I thought so. Be careful. And stay out of sight."

"You, too."

Cody nodded. "I will."

Part of his heart kept insisting he shouldn't let her go by herself. Another part countered with the certainty that he'd be a lot more levelheaded once they were apart. Clear thinking was critical. Everything else was secondary, at least until they figured out what was going on.

Rocks the size of footballs, and smaller, lay hidden

beneath the dead leaves littering the forest floor. Cody picked his way carefully. By peering through the trees he could catch reassuring glimpses of Trudy Lynn now and then. Every time he did, his heart responded by hammering harder.

Struggling to keep up a pace equal to hers, he lost sight of her until he rounded the far corner of the greenhouse. There she was! He raised the cane to signal and saw her wave back as he took a step.

Suddenly, something hit his ankle. Raked across it. Sent pain shooting up his leg.

Arms flailing wildly, Cody twisted his body to protect his injured knee and hit the ground on his side. Hard.

As he fell, the world around him exploded. Green leaves above were riddled and shredded. Bits of bark rained down like dusty hail. The blast echoed across the hills like the rumble of thunder.

Cody clung to the ground. The knifing pain across his ankle told him he must have stumbled over a trip wire that had set off a booby trap. Were there more? There *must* be.

He raised on one elbow before the dust had settled and shouted to Trudy Lynn. "Don't move. Stay where you are."

"What happened? Did somebody shoot at us?"

The quaver in her voice touched his heart. "No. I fell over a wire or something. Don't worry. I'm okay."

"You don't sound okay. Where are you?"

Cody could tell she was drawing nearer despite his warning. "Stand still!" he shouted. "I'll come to you."

In the confusion he'd lost the cane, so he worked himself up a hickory, hand over hand, till he could regain his balance. Gall rose in his throat. The trunk of an adjoining oak bore scars from the basketball-sized shotgun blast. It had struck at eye level. Right where his head should have been—would have been—if he hadn't fallen!

The urge to reach Trudy Lynn and protect her from the same unthinkable threat overpowered him. No pain registered. No rational thought reached his consciousness. All he cared about was getting to her. Before it was too late.

Trudy Lynn saw movement ahead, about where Cody should have been. Was he really all right or had he lied to keep her from coming to his aid?

The latter was most likely. That man was too brave for his own good. And way too bossy. She wasn't helpless, nor was she foolish. These hills were her home. She could tell natural plants and rock formations from anything artificial. If there was a trap set in her path she'd be able to spot it early and avoid it. In that respect, she was probably safer moving around those woods than Cody was.

"No. *You* stay where *you* are. I'm coming," she shouted.

Dropping into a crouch she started to inch forward while carefully perusing the leaf-strewn forest floor. Every sense was heightened. Every muscle tense. Her temples throbbed in time with her rapid pulse and her stomach lurched, bringing bitterness to the back of her throat.

Ahead, she caught glimpses of Cody's blue T-shirt.

He was moving, too! The thought of losing him tore at her heart. She didn't care if he wasn't as fond of her as she was of him, she wasn't going to let him continue to risk his life for her sake.

"I said, *stop*," Trudy Lynn screeched angrily. "Freeze. I'm almost there."

Her skin prickled as if a thousand tiny insects were crawling on it. She lifted her foot to take another step. Hesitated. Pulled back. The leaves ahead didn't look quite right. The ridge piled across her path was too even.

Scanning the area she saw no easy way to bypass the strange formation without backtracking. That was out of the question. If she did manage to avoid the trap, assuming it was a trap, Cody would probably blunder into it before she could reach him.

Picking up a piece of a fallen limb she poked gingerly at the leaves. Nothing happened. She bent lower. Probed more forcefully. Still nothing. Oh, well. Sighing, she turned away as she tossed the broken branch aside.

Her eardrums popped. A shock wave knocked her off her feet and sent her sprawling, facedown, into the suspicious leaves. Intense sound followed a split second later. This blast was lower-pitched than the shot Cody had triggered. It reverberated like the growling of angry beasts, ready to devour anyone or anything in their path.

In the background, Trudy Lynn heard a bellow of pain that cut her all the way to the core. *Cody!*

"No!" she shouted, "No!"

Her heart ached. Tears filled her eyes. Cody had been hit. She'd failed him.

Cody yelled when he saw the flash of the ground blast, saw Trudy Lynn go down. Common sense abandoned him. Half hopping, half running, he raced toward her.

"Dear God," he prayed without reservation, "Help her. Don't let anything happen to her. Please!"

In the deepest reaches of his soul he realized he did believe. Disillusionment and disappointment had clouded his faith but its basic tenets remained. He was the one who had given up. God hadn't.

He saw Trudy raise her head and look at him. Tears streaked her face. Her lips were quivering.

Cody closed the remaining distance and threw himself down beside her, gathering her into his arms. "Oh, honey." Unshed tears blurred his vision. He didn't try to hide his overwhelming relief. "I was afraid… Did it hurt you?"

She clung to him. "I don't think so. Are—are you okay?"

"I'm fine." He tightened his grip and stroked her hair, brushing away crushed leaves and other blast residue. "That was close. Why didn't you stop like I told you to?"

"Because I thought I'd be able to spot traps better than you would." She rested her forehead against his and sighed. "Guess not, huh?"

"No, I guess not."

"You can let go of me." She sounded unconvinced.

"I don't know if I'll ever let you go again."

He realized his confession had flustered her when she quipped, "We'd get awfully hungry and dirty if we stayed out here for the rest of our lives."

"Yeah. I suppose you're right." Slowly, reluctantly, he got to his feet and gave her a hand up. "All we have to do is figure out how to get ourselves out of this mine-field in one piece."

"After we rescue Jim. Don't forget him."

"I'd like to," Cody said, grimacing and staring at the greenhouse. "He's quieted down. Probably figures who-ever set off those traps is history."

"I suppose so." Her brow wrinkled. "If there was anyone else in there, don't you think they'd have come out to investigate? We didn't exactly sneak up on them."

"We sure didn't. Okay. You stay here and wait for me. I'll work my way over there and see who or what's in the greenhouse."

Trudy Lynn latched onto his hand. "Oh, no, you don't. You're not going anywhere without me."

"Yes, I am. I'll have enough to do keeping myself out of trouble. I don't need to be worrying about you, too."

"Fine. Don't worry. But don't think you're going to get away without me again. We split up once and look what happened."

"If we'd been together, one or both of us could have been killed. Use your head. What makes more sense, a small target or a big one?"

"I'm not real fond of becoming either."

Cody was about to continue arguing when he heard

a disturbance in the distance. Leaves were rustling. Dry twigs were snapping. One quick glance at Trudy Lynn's widening eyes told him she'd heard it, too.

She tightened her grip on his fingers. "That's the noise I heard down by the river. It's coming this way!"

"I know." Cody stepped forward and pushed her behind him. The forest was silent except for the approaching threat. Jim chose that moment to let out a howl that would have made a demented hyena proud.

An enormous ebony shape burst from the brush and charged at them.

Trudy Lynn started to scream, then choked it off when she recognized the beast.

Sailor gamboled up and shook himself, sending a shower of river water and forest refuse in all directions.

Jim cut loose with another heartrending wail.

Sailor's ears perked up. His big head swiveled, nose pointing to the greenhouse, hackles raised.

"Easy, boy," Cody said. "It's okay."

Sailor apparently disagreed because he sprang into action and made a beeline for the plastic-covered structure.

Cody shouted, "No!" in unison with Trudy Lynn.

The Newfoundland ignored them both. In seconds, he'd reached the side of the plastic-covered structure and made his own door by charging through the flimsy wall as if it were tissue paper.

"Follow that dog," Trudy Lynn said, tugging on Cody's hand. "If he made it safely, we can, too."

* * *

Trudy Lynn shinnied through the Newf-sized hole ahead of Cody. The sight that greeted her inside was so funny she couldn't help laughing in spite of the seriousness of the situation.

Jim was tied to a toppled chair and lying on his back, feet kicking in the air. Sailor stood over him, lapping his face, while he sputtered and cursed.

Green fronds on thick, segmented stalks were everywhere, some growing, some stacked in bundles after a recent harvest. The air was humid, cloying, with a pungent trace of wet dog.

"Come on, boy," Trudy Lynn said, tugging on Sailor's collar to ease him away. "That's clean enough. We'll let you wash him off again later if you want."

Jim was blubbering. "Get that monster off me."

"You don't want to be rescued?"

"Not by *that*." He spit. "Untie me."

Cody joined Trudy Lynn to look down on the captive youth. "Not so fast," he said. "Your cousin and I almost got ourselves killed out there. Before we let you loose I'd like to know just what we've stumbled into."

"Oh, like you don't know," Jim grumbled. "Give me a break, man. Everybody knows marijuana when they see it. What'd you think all this stuff was, okra?"

"The question is, who tied you up and why?"

"Never mind that. Just get me out of here before they come back."

"They, who? Buford's out of commission. Who else should we look out for?"

"What happened to him?" Jim was clearly frightened.

Cody chuckled and elbowed Trudy Lynn. "Some woman who doesn't know her own strength gave him a bad headache. He's stuck in the hospital for observation but he'll be released soon. I suggest you cut the macho act and start talking. Otherwise, we may decide to leave you right where you are."

"You wouldn't."

"Maybe. Maybe not," Cody drawled. "I don't think you want to take that chance, do you?"

"No." Jim's glare was hard, then softened as it settled on his cousin. "I really was trying to help you, Trudy Lynn. They said they'd hurt you if I didn't get you to sell or make you close down."

Incredulous, she shook her head slowly. "Why couldn't you have confided in me? I'd have helped you."

"Who says I wanted help? I had a sweet deal—" his glance shifted back to Cody "—till *he* showed up and ruined everything."

"In that case, we'll be going." Trudy Lynn took Cody's arm.

"No! Wait! I'm sorry. I didn't mean it." Tears filled the younger man's eyes. "Take me with you. Buford'll kill us all if he finds you here. This is his biggest crop yet. He'll do anything to protect it."

Cody's jaw muscles clenched. "I don't doubt that. He nearly blew us up out there."

"That's why you need me. I can guide you back to the river. I know all the safe trails. I can't believe you made it this far." Tears were streaming out the corners of his eyes and dripping into his ears. "Please? For Mamaw's sake?"

"That does it," Trudy Lynn told Cody. "Poor Earlene deserves to get him back in one piece, even if he isn't worth half as much as her little finger."

"If you say so." Cody found a pair of lopping shears and cut the ropes.

Jim stood stiffly, sniffled and rubbed his chafed wrists. Sailor had edged between him and the other two. Jim eyed the dog. "Is he gonna bite me?"

"Not as long as you behave yourself," Cody said soberly.

Trudy Lynn hid her face and stifled a snicker. That big moose was about as likely to bite as Widget was to become a cuddly lapdog. Of course, letting Jim believe Sailor might attack was advantageous, especially since they had no defensive weapons other than the dog's teeth.

Give me a canoe paddle anytime, Trudy Lynn mused. She was immediately penitent. *Sorry, Lord. I do love my neighbors. Honest, I do.*

Her thoughts broadened to include Cody Keringhoven. Now there was a neighbor she could easily learn to love.

Learn to? Hah! Who was she kidding? She was already so smitten with the man she could hardly think straight, let alone function when he was around. She cared so much for him it hurt to even think about it.

And that's not all, she added ruefully. *He's going to get well, just like I prayed he would, and then he's going to leave. He's much better already. It won't be long before he goes back to California.*

That thought was enough to bring a lump to her throat and threaten tears. She blinked them back and squared her shoulders. California was where Cody longed to be, where he should be. Running rapids was his life. Weeks ago he'd been ready to give up and now look at him! Resuming the career he loved was going to provide the incentive to make a full recovery and she wasn't going to do anything to ruin that. Not even confess that she was falling in love with him.

FIFTEEN

Cody used a piece of the rope from Jim's bindings as a makeshift leash. Sailor tolerated the restraint, though he plodded along looking thoroughly dejected. Jim was in the lead, followed by Trudy Lynn. Cody and his dog brought up the rear.

"Is Sailor sulking?" Trudy Lynn asked over her shoulder.

Cody chuckled. "I think so. He's used to being able to choose his own path. I couldn't let him do that here."

"No kidding." She lowered her voice and slowed to speak privately. "What are we going to do with you-know-who?"

"Now or later?"

"Either. I suppose he'll be safer if he's in jail."

"I'd say so. We know there'll be a raid on the greenhouse ASAP. Then the fur will really start to fly."

"That's true. How's your leg?"

"Not too bad. I know it's there."

"You seem to be doing a lot better."

Cody huffed. "Better than what?"

"Better than when you first came to Serenity. I'm amazed."

"I'm a little surprised, too. The doctors told me I might need arthroscopic surgery eventually. Right now, I'm just glad to be on my feet again."

"I'm happy for you," Trudy Lynn said, smiling back at him. "I was afraid you'd given up."

"On what?"

"Everything."

"Oh." Cody let his thoughts ramble as he kept pace. There was plenty of truth to her observation. Although his irrational anger had dissipated, he still nurtured a modicum of disillusionment. It was getting harder and harder, however, to pinpoint his problem, to give it a name and face. For one thing, he'd stopped blaming Stephanie for jilting him and was seeing their breakup in a new light. What if he'd married her? What a tragedy that would have been. He'd not only have taken sacred vows to honor her as his wife, he'd have been unable to freely enjoy Trudy Lynn's companionship.

That's what he and his sister's best friend were, Cody decided easily. Companions. They'd gone from being mere acquaintances to being good friends in less time than it had taken him to convince Stephanie to accept their first date!

Which proves what? Cody asked himself. That he really was meant to be there? Meant to meet Trudy Lynn? Meant to come to her aid? Well, why not? How else could he explain their harmony of thoughts and feelings, the way they argued, yet always ended up on the same side?

Cody smiled. He wasn't ready to call their meeting of the minds divinely inspired, but it certainly had been interesting so far. He could hardly wait to see what happened next.

Jim halted at the shore of a brackish green backwater, just upstream from where Trudy Lynn and Cody had beached their canoe. A beat-up bass boat was moored to a stump. The only thing new about it was its powerful outboard motor.

"We can take this," Jim said, grabbing the rope at the boat's bow and tugging it closer. "It'll make good time."

Trudy Lynn's brow furrowed. "Will we all fit?"

"Sure. No sweat," the younger man assured her. "Buford and I haul…" He seemed to think better of it. "Never mind. Just get in."

"Sailor, too," Trudy Lynn insisted. "I'm not going anywhere without him."

Jim cursed under his breath. "Let him walk."

"He could swim the way he must have when he followed us," Cody offered. "He's never been in a boat before. I'm not sure how he'll act."

"He'll be fine." She was adamant. "We'd still be stuck in the woods, wondering if we were going to be blown to bits with every step, if it hadn't been for him." She looked to Cody for confirmation, then stepped into the boat, sat to one side and patted the bench seat. "Come on, boy."

The Newfoundland shifted its feet in a nervous dance, acting unsure, until Cody said, "Okay," and released the tension on the improvised leash. Sailor leaped into the boat beside Trudy Lynn as if he'd been trained to do so.

The dog's momentum pushed the stern away from the bank and made the whole craft rock wildly. Trudy Lynn laughed and hugged the dog's neck. "Whoa! That was some jump. I thought you said he didn't know how to handle himself around boats."

"It must be a genetic talent," Cody answered. He waded knee deep to pull the port side of the craft parallel to the sandy shore. "You two stay where you are. Don't make any more waves. Jim and I'll get in the back by the motor."

Cody swung aboard and inched to the starboard side. "Okay, Jim. I'm set. Climb in."

The younger man shook his head, his eyes wide and frightened, his fists clenched. "No way. I ain't ridin' with that monster."

"You don't have a choice," Cody said. "You either ride with him or he has you for lunch. It's your call."

It was the tears welling in her cousin's eyes that spurred Trudy Lynn to suggest, "Maybe Jim could sit in our canoe and we could tow him behind."

"If we knew where it was," Cody said. "Got any idea?"

"Yes. I think it's right down there." She pointed. "Jim can walk along the bank to get it while we follow."

One of Cody's eyebrows arched quizzically. "You trust him that far?"

"Of course I do," she said sweetly. "If he tries to run you can always sic your man-eating beast on him." She had to turn away and bite her lower lip to keep from giggling. Now that the worst was over she was giddy with relief.

"That should work. I haven't fed him today."

His quip was almost too much for her. She pressed her fingertips to her mouth. Her shoulders shook. Laughter threatened to bubble out, as unstoppable as the Spring River emerging from Mammoth Spring.

Cody saved the situation by saying, "I know you're upset, Trudy Lynn, but don't cry. It'll be all right."

She kept her face averted and nodded silently. Cody was right about one thing. Tears were running down her cheeks. Only they weren't from sadness, they were from the pleasure of being there with him. Of sharing another private joke, a moment of joy meant only for them.

Nothing could ever steal the memories of this amazing encounter from her. Not even the passage of time.

Sniffling, she regained a shaky bit of self-control and began to lecture herself. She had a million things to be thankful for. It was wrong to brood. Wrong to borrow trouble. And wrong to anticipate missing Cody when he was still there.

His warning to not rock the boat took on a deeper meaning. She wouldn't make waves, wouldn't upset him when he was in such high spirits. And if—when—he left her, she'd wave goodbye and smile no matter how much her heart was breaking. He'd rescued her from her troubles. The least she could do was see that he triumphed over his, as well.

* * *

Becky and Logan were among the crowd gathered at the county line landing when Jim was finally taken into custody. Will was there with Jim's weeping grandmother, Earlene. A few straggling reporters had heard the police dispatch on their scanners and had shown up, too.

Becky hugged Trudy Lynn, then led her far from the newshounds who had begun to pester the sheriff for details.

Logan shook hands with Cody and thumped him on the back as they walked away. "Good job, man."

"Thanks." Cody was beginning to feel the strain. "I'm glad it's over." He felt a gentle nudge and reached down to pet Sailor.

"Did the kid explain where he was all this time?"

Cody nodded. "Yeah. He was skipping out on Trudy Lynn and me when he first disappeared. His cohorts decided he was too big a risk to have running around loose, so they tied him up till they could decide what to do with him."

"Sounds like Jim was lucky you found him."

"That's what the sheriff said." He looked back at the harried lawman. "I'm glad those reporters are leaving us alone. I've just about had it with their stupid questions."

"I imagine you have. How's Trudy Lynn doing?"

"Okay, I guess." Cody took a deep breath and released it as a sigh. "We almost got killed out there. I was never so scared in my life."

"But you made it through," Logan said quietly.

"I don't know how." Cody blinked back telltale moisture. "If Sailor hadn't shown up when he did we'd probably still be looking for a safe escape route."

Staring into the distance and focused on nothing in particular, Cody began to speak as if he were narrating a documentary. "I'd nearly had my head blown off by a booby trap. Trudy Lynn wouldn't listen to me. I told her to stop. To freeze. To let me make the next move. But she just kept coming. And then…" His voice cracked with emotion.

Logan rested a hand on his shoulder. "It's okay. Take your time."

"I heard this terrible explosion. I saw her fall. I thought…" A tear slid down Cody's cheek. He quickly wiped it away. "I thought I'd lost her."

"What did you do then?"

He shrugged. "I don't know, exactly. I remember running to her." His gaze shifted to Logan. "I think I was praying."

"And your prayers were answered."

"Before I asked. Sailor was already on his way. Guess I was wasting my time, huh?"

"Not at all." Logan smiled. "The important thing is that you proved you haven't lost your faith. If you had, you wouldn't have turned to God when the going got rough. Deep in your heart, you trusted Him to help you."

Cody was shaking his head. "I don't know why I should have. He didn't answer my prayers when my passenger and I were tossed into those rapids."

"Didn't He?"

"No. My client died. Drowned."

Logan was nodding. "I'd figured as much." He paused, then went on sympathetically. "We all tend to put the same limits on God that we experience as human beings. Because we can't look ahead and see what's in store, we forget that He knows our future, knows what's best for us. In spite of the fact we may disagree with God's answers to our prayers, they're still answers, even if we don't understand them at the time."

"I'll never understand why that kid had to drown. He was just starting to live."

"I don't have the answer to that, either," Logan said.

"So, I'm supposed to just trust? Blindly? Is that what you're saying?"

"Why not? You do it all the time." He gestured with a sweep of his arm. "Look around us. You breathe the air because you sense that it's here and you need it, yet you can't see it. You assume morning will come when you close your eyes to sleep because it always has."

"There's more to it than that."

"Of course there is. There's more to God and His universe than any mortal will ever be able to comprehend. We think we're geniuses when we supposedly figure out one tiny secret. Then, years later, somebody else comes along and contradicts what was once considered a brilliant discovery and proves it was wrong. All any of us can do is muddle through." Logan smiled. "I've chosen to do it by following the Lord's teachings as best I can."

Cody sighed again. "I used to feel the same way."

"Search your heart," the preacher said. "See what's in there now. Be honest with yourself. You may be surprised."

"Surprised? Hah! I've been astonished by just about everything that's happened since I hit town. One more amazing thing will fall right in line with the rest."

"Around here, they call that being *bumfuzzled*. Becky tells me it means you're so bewildered and confused you're practically speechless."

Cody chuckled quietly and glanced across the parking lot to where Trudy Lynn and Becky stood. They were obviously rejoicing over the turn of the day's events and, as usual, Trudy's voice carried best.

"That's one thing my landlady doesn't have to worry about," Cody said wryly. "No matter how bumfuzzled she gets, she's never speechless."

Trudy Lynn pressed her fingertips to her temples. "What an adventure. I hope I never have one like it again." She gave Becky a smile of heartfelt appreciation. "I'm so glad you and Logan came to meet us. I need a friend, especially right now."

"I'm here for you, kiddo. Would you like to spend the night at our house? I know Logan wouldn't mind."

"Widget would," Trudy Lynn said. "He's probably been driving poor Annie crazy while I've been gone. Besides, he'll need me there tonight to let him out."

"You could just have Cody's dog take care of it for you," Becky joked. "He seems to love opening doors."

"Or running right through them. You should have

seen him go charging into that greenhouse after Jim hollered for help. He was a real hero."

"I thought Cody was your hero."

"Okay, him, too." She blushed. "I'm going to miss him."

"Why? Did he say he was leaving?"

"No, but…"

"Then stop borrowing trouble. He's made enormous progress since he's arrived. Maybe he'll decide to stay."

"Why should he?"

"I don't know. Can't you think of a good reason?" Becky grinned. One eyebrow arched. "I can."

"Don't look at me like that. There's nothing going on between your brother and me." The corners of her mouth twitched with a repressed smile. "Well, almost nothing."

"Aha! I knew it."

"Knew what? There's nothing to know. Cody and I are good friends, that's all."

"You're sure?"

"Yes."

"Positive?"

Trudy Lynn's voice rose. "Yes, already!"

"How many times has he kissed you?"

"Twice," she blurted, then began waving her hands like a kitten that had just accidentally stepped in a bowl of milk. "It's not like that. Once didn't even count. I was talking and he was only trying to shut me up." Her brow furrowed. "Wait. Maybe that was the third time. I don't remember exactly."

"You do so," Becky challenged.

"Okay. So he kissed me twice and I may have kissed him once, besides. It was my idea that time but it doesn't count either. I was only thanking him for saving my life."

"You could have done that by baking him some oatmeal raisin cookies," Becky countered.

Trudy Lynn quirked a smile and shook her head. "No, I couldn't have. I had to kiss him."

"Oh? Why is that?"

"Because I'm out of raisins. Used the last one on my cereal the other day."

Cody heard the pleasant sound of Trudy's Lynn's laughter and smiled in response.

"Sounds like our ladies are unwinding," Logan said.

"Yeah. I hope they're not laughing about us."

"Shall we join them and find out?"

"In a minute." Cody paused to clear his throat. "You counsel people, don't you?"

"Yes. If you want to talk more privately we can schedule an appointment in my office."

"I don't want to take up your time. I just had a couple of questions."

"About God?"

"No." Cody huffed and chuckled. "Something much harder to understand. Women."

Logan laughed with him and clapped him on the back. "Terrific. Why couldn't you have asked me to explain how long eternity lasts or why the world seems to be such a confusing mess these days? That, I could handle."

"That's too easy," Cody joked. "Why should I make this painless for you when I'm suffering."

"You want me to share your pain?"

"Something like that."

"Then I take it this isn't a rhetorical discussion. Remember, as Trudy Lynn's pastor I can't reveal anything told to me in confidence."

"Of course not. I wouldn't expect you to. I just wonder if you think it's possible to fall in love in a few weeks?"

"It was for Becky and me," Logan said. "Then again, people make mistakes about their feelings all the time."

"I know. I've done it. I guess what I'm asking is, do you think Trudy Lynn would settle for someone like me?" The question came out sounding too negative to suit Cody. He was about to rephrase it when Logan answered, "No."

Cody's heart fell. "I see."

"No, you don't," Logan said flatly. "She's not the type to settle for anything except what she really wants. That's why I think she'd *choose* a man like you." He began to grin. "And if you're planning to ask her how she feels, I suggest you phrase it more tactfully than you just did or she's liable to stomp off in a huff."

"That's her usual reaction to everything I say."

"This time it won't be," Logan advised.

"I don't want to rush her and scare her away. I've never met anyone half as wonderful as Trudy Lynn. I intend to stay right here and spend the rest of my life making her happy."

"Well, I'm sold," Logan gibed. "And judging by the

way you two have been staring at each other ever since we got here, I'd say she is, too."

"I want it to be special for her when I propose. Really romantic. Women like that."

"If you're such an expert, why did you have to ask for my advice?"

"Maybe I wanted to humor you," Cody suggested. "After all, you are my brother-in-law. And the pastor of the woman I love. If she comes to you for guidance, I want to be sure you know my intentions are honorable."

"I never doubted that for a minute," Logan said. "Come on. Becky and I'll give you a lift back to camp. If you're planning on a romantic evening you're definitely going to need to shower and shave." He wrinkled up his nose. "It might be wise to wash that dog of yours, too. I'm not sure which one of you smells worse."

"Thanks for the confidence boost," Cody teased. "It was just what I needed."

"Hey, that's what spiritual advisors are for."

"So, how are you going to get us home?" Cody glanced down at his damp, muddy, canine companion. "In the backseat of your car?"

"I sincerely hope not. I think I saw Will in the crowd. He's probably driving the camp truck. Sailor can ride with him." Logan gave Cody the once-over. "Come to think of it, you might want to, too. So the dog doesn't worry, I mean."

Cody laughed heartily. "Smooth, Logan. Very smooth. We'll work something out." He gestured toward the women. "Let's go."

Falling into step beside him, Logan asked, "What's the hurry? Is your leg bothering you."

"No worse than usual. I just want to get back to Trudy Lynn. We've been apart long enough."

"Oh, man, you do have it bad, don't you?" Logan was laughing softly and shaking his head. "I'll pray for you."

"While you're at it, you might want to pray for Trudy Lynn, too," Cody said. "The most important thing to me is that she be happy. Understand?"

"With or without you, you mean?"

Cody nodded soberly. "Exactly."

Buford scowled at the wall-mounted pay phone and squeezed the receiver till his knuckles whitened. "No. I'm still in the county hospital. They're supposed to be lettin' me out soon."

"So, what's your problem?"

"The sheriff's been to see me. Twice. He and I go way back but I don't like the way he looked at me the last time he was here. Somethin's up. I can feel it."

"There better not be any glitches. I've got a bundle invested in your operation."

"Then you'd best have my bail ready."

"Think you'll need it?"

He snorted in disgust. "Who knows?"

"What about the kid? Is he going to keep his mouth shut?"

Buford cackled. "Oh, yeah. I've got that covered. Little Jimmy's not gonna be a bit of trouble. Matter of fact, if I don't get out of here soon he may start singin' with the heavenly choir."

A string of curses erupted on the other end of the line. "What do you mean? I told you to keep this operation clean."

"Except for the woman."

"Yeah. And that old man who works for her. I wouldn't mind if Will had an accident."

"What about her boyfriend?"

The cursing intensified. "If you have to get rough, start with him. Think you can handle it?"

"'Course I can."

"You sure? He put you in the hospital once."

"Did not!" Buford growled into the phone. "It was that woman. She hit me from behind, when I wasn't lookin'. It won't happen again."

"Good. See that it doesn't. And if you do get arrested, call that bail-bondsman in Searcy, the one we used before. I'll leave word with him that I guarantee your bond."

"Hey, thanks, Mr—"

"Shut up! I've told you never to use my name. Anybody could be listening."

"That's why I'm usin' the pay phone in the hall," Buford said, scowling. "Don't worry. Your secret's safe with me. I ain't told a soul who you are." He cackled. "Sure would like to, though. Give 'em a real surprise."

"No one who works with you knows who your backer is?"

"Nope. Nary a soul. 'Specially not Jimmy-boy."

"Good. See that it stays that way."

"Yes, sir."

"And Buford?"

"Yeah?"

"The kid stays alive. I don't know what you had in mind for him but forget it. Earlene's a nice old lady. She doesn't deserve to have to bury her grandson."

"I'll do my best."

"Do better than that."

"I don't know. If I go straight to jail from here it could put me in a bind. I left him…" There was a loud click on the line. "Hello? Hello?"

Buford held the receiver in front of his face and stared at it in disbelief. His benefactor had hung up on him! Just like that. As if he didn't matter any more than a cockroach crawling up a wall. Well, he'd see about that. When all this was over, Mister High-and-Mighty was gonna get his comeuppance. Yes, sirree.

But first, he had a job to do. If Jimmy hadn't died of fright or thirst by now, he was going to let him go. If it was too late, then the kid would just disappear for keeps. Either way was fine with him.

Determined, he headed for the nearest room to look for some street clothes he could steal.

SIXTEEN

Will had escorted Earlene to the river landing so she could see for herself that Jim was alive and well. Trudy Lynn had felt she'd be intruding if she rode home with the older couple, so she'd asked Becky and Logan to give her a lift while Cody and Sailor hitched a chilly ride back to camp in the bed of Will's pickup.

Trudy Lynn had had to drag herself through evening chores. When she'd completed the absolute minimum she'd showered and collapsed into a deck chair on her porch.

Widget had been acting miffed ever since she'd returned. He started sniffing her shoes again, stiff-legged and hackles raised, when she finally took time to relax.

"Don't look at me like that," Trudy Lynn said with a smile. "I *had* to associate with Sailor. And I'm going to do it again, so you'd better get used to it."

The little terrier cocked its head and pricked its ears, obviously listening.

"You do understand, don't you? That's good. Because maybe you can explain everything to me."

She sighed. Deeply. Poignantly. Empathetic, the little dog jumped into her lap and rested his front paws on her shoulders, straining to lick her face.

Trudy Lynn held him away and smiled. "No kisses, baby. But thanks for forgiving me. I need a buddy like you right now. I'm really mixed-up."

Wiggling, Widget struggled to be let go.

"Okay, okay. I know you don't like to cuddle." She turned him sideways so he could sit comfortably in her lap and began to gently stroke his back to calm him. "Humor me and settle down, will you? Please? That's a good boy."

Another sigh whooshed out. "It's all over, Widget. Jim's safe in jail, where he belongs, and Will's commiserating with Earlene. If he doesn't waste this chance, he might actually have someone special to spend the rest of his life with, which is more than I have to look forward to at the moment."

The little dog shifted, wiggled, tried again to lick her and managed one quick swipe at the underside of her chin. She giggled. "Yes, I love you, too, even if you are too full of yourself to be endearing like a certain Newfie I could mention."

Thoughts of Sailor's easygoing temperament reminded her of his master. Some experts insisted that people chose dogs to complement their own personalities. In Cody's case, that might have been truer in the past. He had seemed laid-back and pretty carefree before he'd been injured. Now, it was hard to tell what he was feeling. Too bad she wasn't as intuitive about his thoughts as Widget was about hers.

Then again, she wasn't sure she wanted to know what Cody was really thinking. She might not like what she learned. She'd already tried to tell him how much she cared for him and he'd reacted like a bear trying to sidestep the jaws of a poacher's trap. Well, fine. She could wait a little longer to find out whether or not he was still planning to go back to California.

Or could she? Day after day of not knowing had left her so jittery she babbled incessantly every time she was near him. He'd made jokes about how much she talked but he had to be getting weary of it just the same.

"What would you do to get Cody to pay attention to you, Widget? Huh?" Trudy Lynn giggled. "Never mind. You'd probably growl at him or bite his ankle."

So, what was she going to do? *Nothing? Something? The wrong thing?* Probably the latter. When it came to Cody Keringhoven she seemed to stick her foot in her mouth on a regular basis.

"He'd say that's because my mouth is always open to talk," Trudy Lynn muttered. Well, when he was right, he was right. It was in her nature to express herself. Period. Even if she did manage to subdue the urge long enough to favorably impress him, she'd be creating an erroneous image of herself. That wouldn't be fair. If he liked her—even loved her—it should be because of her real self, not some pretend personality she'd created for his benefit.

She'd told Cody he'd be denying God's ultimate wisdom if he refused to accept himself. Now that she thought about it, that was good advice for her, too.

Her eyes closed. "Thank you, Father. I am glad to be me. And I'm glad You sent Cody into my life, even if he isn't going to stay."

She had so much more to be grateful for it was overwhelming. Memories of blessings cascaded through her mind like a raft racing down whitewater rapids. The Lord had taken care of her when her mother had died and her father had offered little emotional support. He'd sent her Will when she'd needed a good hand. He'd removed Ned to keep her from listening to the urging of friends and marrying the wrong man. And He'd revealed Jim's delinquency in time to not only save him from himself but to rescue her business.

Those things, and more, reinforced her optimism about the future. All she had to do was trust God as she had before, rely on His wisdom and get out of His way.

That notion brought a smile. She did trust the Lord. It was letting go and stepping back so He could work, unhindered, that had always been so hard for her.

"And keeping my mouth shut," she added, giving Widget a hug. "Think I can ever learn to do that?"

She giggled as the terrier jumped down and began circling her feet. "There's about as much chance of me being quiet as there is of you sitting still."

Widget was barking. Trudy Lynn opened heavy-lidded eyes. Lightning flashed in the distant night sky. The only other illumination was from red and blue lights atop a patrol car outside her window. How long had she been asleep? What time was it? And how long had it been raining?

She squinted at the illuminated digital clock by her bedside: 2:00 a.m. Terrific. If she ever got a good night's rest she wouldn't know what to do with all the extra energy.

Getting up, she pulled a terry cloth robe over her pajamas, fastened it, then bent to pick up her little dog. Widget was always on edge in stormy weather. The last thing she needed was for him to get overexcited and nip an innocent police officer.

Trudy Lynn unlocked the kitchen door, opened it a crack and peered out. She recognized the dripping deputy standing under the porch light and relaxed. "Hi, Nathan. Want to come in out of the rain? I can make some fresh coffee."

"Evening, Trudy Lynn." When he nodded and touched the brim of his hat, the water poured off its plastic cover. "I'll have to take a rain check on that coffee. We're real busy tonight. Sheriff sent me over here to tell you Buford's on the loose. He walked out of the hospital. Nobody missed him till shift change."

"Surely, he won't come here."

"We don't think so, either, 'specially not if he's on foot. It's too far. Just being on the safe side. Take care and lock up, okay?" He touched his hat brim again. "Night."

"Good night. And thanks."

Widget growled menacingly as the deputy turned and headed for his car.

"Atta boy," Trudy Lynn said. "You protect me."

After watching the police cruiser roll out of camp she

stepped back, closed and locked the door. Most of her cabins were empty after the mass exodus of reporters plus all the vacation cancellations. But Will was here. And Cody. They should be warned, too.

She put Widget down and hurriedly picked up the phone. There was no dial tone. "That figures. One little storm and everything quits working. As usual."

The little dog bristled. Concerned, Trudy Lynn watched him sniff the floor, then closely investigate the door she'd just locked. He was growling. His body stiffened, every muscle tense as if he were ready for an attack. When he pawed the door and whined she was positive something was wrong. Widget hated getting wet. He never asked to go out in bad weather. Never.

"That does it. Come on, boy."

Knowing he'd follow, she flipped off the kitchen lights, dashed down the hall to the rear of the camp store, and snatched up the phone there. *Dead as a doornail!*

Apprehensive, she ducked behind the sales counter. What now? She couldn't reach the panel controlling the overnight lighting in the store without passing the display windows. If she did that, anyone watching could spot her. But what else could she do? How else could she hide?

A silent prayer flickered through her subconscious. The bedroom! Her cell phone was in her purse in the bedroom! She stroked Widget. He was trembling as he always did during thunderstorms but he'd ceased growling. That was a good sign.

She got an extra jolt of energy when the electricity

fluttered, then failed. Lunging toward the doorway, she would have fallen over her dog if he hadn't been so agile.

Together they tore down the dark hallway, Widget's claws scratching the bare floor like mice scrambling to escape a cat. At least the lights wouldn't give her away. If Buford was responsible for the power outage he'd made a big mistake. Darkness was to her advantage.

She caught her bare toes on the leading edge of a crocheted rug and stumbled. Trying to regain her balance she reached for the doorjamb. All she grabbed was empty air! Her ankle wrenched. Her body jerked forward.

Widget yipped a warning at the last second. Trudy Lynn twisted to one side, barely missing him, and landed with a thud that echoed throughout the entire lodge building.

She lay still for a moment and took stock of the situation. Her head and arms were fine. Her back hurt but not terribly. So did her hip. When it came to her right ankle, however, there was no question that she had a problem. The slightest movement sent arrows of pain shooting up her leg.

She bit her lip to keep from crying out. Where, exactly, was she? How much farther to her purse? Had she put it in its usual place or had she gotten careless?

A tiny green light flashed three times near the floor. Then another answered. A couple of fireflies must have slipped inside when she'd opened the door to talk to Nathan! The little bugs weren't giving much light but their rhythmic flashes were enough to confirm that she was in the bedroom.

She held her breath and waited for the next series of green winks. There? Yes! Her purse! She must have knocked it to the floor when she'd been startled awake by the deputy.

Widget was crowding close. "It's okay, boy," she whispered. "Back off. Go on."

He refused to leave her side. Trudy Lynn gritted her teeth and pulled herself across the floor on her elbows. She had to reach her cell phone. It was her only lifeline.

Nausea forced her to pause three times before she reached her goal. Tears trickled down her cheeks, unnoticed till Widget tried to lick them off. His attempts at comfort helped her focus on something besides the knifing pain.

"It's okay, sweetie. We'll be fine. This is one time I wish you were a lot bigger and meaner, though."

It took several seconds, several more shuddering breaths, before she could steady her hands enough to retrieve the small cellular telephone and dial 911.

The dispatcher told her to stay on the line till help arrived. Trudy Lynn was far too preoccupied to comply. If all the landlines in camp were out she knew she couldn't warn Will, but there must be something she could do.

Her heart jumped like a grasshopper on a hot sidewalk. *Cody has a cell phone.* She wasn't helpless after all! Or was she? What was Cody's number? Had he written it down and given it to her? If so, where had she put it?

Frustration bred tears. She sniffled. *Stupid, stupid, stupid. Think. Better yet, pray.*

She desperately wanted to call out to God, yet it seemed there was nothing left inside her but pain. And fear.

Cheeks bathed in tears, she pulled the little dog into her arms, held him tight and counted the seconds.

Sailor was restless. So was Cody. He'd seen the police car leaving after Sailor had barked him awake. Local law enforcement had been keeping the place under pretty close surveillance ever since Jim's disappearance, so the visit wasn't unusual. Still, it was disquieting. Jim was in jail and Buford would be arrested soon, if he wasn't already in custody, so why continue the patrol?

Scowling, Cody paced to the window and peered through the drizzle at the lodge. Trudy Lynn was up there. Since there were no lights burning in her quarters he figured she must be sleeping, which was what he'd be doing if he had good sense.

Standing beside him, Sailor growled so deeply Cody felt the vibration of the dog's rib cage against his leg. That did it. He was going to get dressed and hike up the hill if it killed him. And if there was no sign Trudy Lynn was awake when he got there, he and Sailor would spend the rest of the night camped on her porch, standing guard. If she thought that was usurping too much control over her life, they could argue about it in the morning.

He pulled on jeans and a T-shirt, then grabbed his hooded jacket, thankful it was waterproof. His cell phone was in the pocket. He took it out, held it for a moment, then decided against calling ahead. No use giving her the opportunity to insist he wasn't needed.

Besides, he admitted, slipping his feet into running shoes, it wasn't Trudy Lynn he was really doing this for. He was the one who needed to see that she was safe, to place himself between her and any threat, real or imagined.

The second he reached for the doorknob Sailor was right there, waiting to poke his nose out first.

"Okay. Tonight you can go," Cody said. "But no barking and waking everybody up. I'll get your leash."

He'd no more than turned when he heard a horrendous splintering. He spun around. The door was hanging at an awkward angle, its lock free of the jamb. From the looks of the damage, Sailor had simply hurled himself against the old wood and taken off. Will's recent repairs hadn't stood a chance of withstanding so much concentrated force.

"Well, that tears it," Cody grumbled. "The whole camp will be awake in a few minutes."

He'd left the porch and was halfway up the hill when the phone in his pocket rang. Answering, he put his back to the wind and used the jacket's hood as a shield. The caller was so agitated he couldn't understand a word at first. "Slow down. Who is this?"

"It's me. Becky. Where are you?"

"In camp. Why?"

"The police were just here. They're looking everywhere for Buford. Somebody must have told him Jim had been arrested and he took off. They don't think he's had time to get as far as the Spring River but I thought I should warn you, anyway."

The back of Cody's neck bristled. "What's Trudy

Lynn's number? Never mind. I'm almost to the lodge. Hang up and call the cops for me. Tell them to get out here in a hurry. Sailor's sure there's a prowler."

Blood was whooshing through the veins in Trudy's Lynn's head so fast it made a humming noise that hampered her hearing. Her temples were throbbing. Her ankle was, too, a quarter beat later. The skin felt drawn. Clearly, her foot and lower leg were starting to swell.

Widget stiffened, cocked his head. Moments later she thought she heard the tinkle of breaking glass. It wasn't loud, like a drinking glass shattering after being dropped onto the floor. It sounded more like one of the small panes in her back door was being tapped out.

She closed her eyes and clung tightly to her little dog. If anyone was searching the place they'd be found. Quickly.

A growl rumbled. Trudy Lynn closed her hand around Widget's pointy muzzle and whispered, "Shush."

Struggling to get loose, the little terrier continued sounding the warning.

She could hear soft footfalls now. A hesitant cadence. Someone had gotten inside! And they were coming closer.

Gritting her teeth she dragged herself farther behind the bed. Beads of perspiration glistened on her forehead and trickled down her spine. This would have to be good enough. She couldn't force herself to move one inch more.

"Easy, boy, easy," she whispered, hoping a soft tone and gentle petting would calm her anxious dog. Every muscle in his body was knotted, ready for action. If he got away from her and attacked the prowler the way he obviously wanted to, there was no telling how badly he'd be hurt. She couldn't let that happen.

A sudden jingling on the floor at the foot of the bed made Trudy Lynn jump. She bit back a gasp. The phone! She'd been so concerned for Widget she must have dropped it. Were the police calling her back? Were they almost there?

A sudden foreboding thought gave her chills. Suppose there had been confusion about who she was or where she was calling from? Had she mentioned the camp? She must have. Besides, the dispatcher had caller ID, right? But would it work with a portable number?

The little phone continued to play the tune she'd programmed into it instead of its normal ring. Music she'd once thought amusing was now mocking. Even if she could convince herself to crawl out of hiding to answer, the caller would probably have hung up by the time she got there. And then she'd be back in the open, a sitting duck.

Yeah. A duck with a broken wing and no way to defend myself, she added, grimacing. There was nothing to do but sit there and wait till the stupid thing finally shut up.

By the sixth repeat of the silly ditty she was ready to smash the phone with anything at hand. Only there wasn't anything at hand. Not even a canoe paddle. If she was so organized and perfectly prepared, why hadn't she put one in her bedroom? That question wasn't as ridiculous as it sounded.

"Because I didn't dream I was going to need a weapon," she whispered. "Not here. Not in Serenity."

The phone fell silent. Listening for footsteps in the background, Trudy Lynn thought she heard two sets, one slow and another faster, lighter. She held her breath. Strained to hear. She'd had to have been wearing earplugs to miss the ensuing groan and heavy thump.

Were the police here? If they were, if they'd captured her prowler, then why didn't somebody turn the electricity back on?

In her arms, Widget's growl intensified till his whole body shook. The beam from a flashlight swept through the door and around the room. It came to rest on the cell phone.

Someone laughed and said, "Well, well." Someone whose voice sounded familiar. Only it couldn't possibly be him.

Soft footfalls approached. The light blinded Trudy Lynn. She blinked and shaded her eyes, trying to see who was really there. Widget had ceased growling and was in full attack mode, barking so fervently he drowned out everything else.

"Still got the rat, I see," the voice said.

That was enough identification for Trudy. She didn't have to see his face to recognize his attitude. "Ned? What're you doing here?"

"Can't I stop by to see my ex-fiancée?"

In spite of the animosity evident in his tone she was glad he'd chosen this particular night to visit. "Listen. There's a prowler in the building. I heard him break in the back door. I think it's that Buford guy from down-river. He's been growing marijuana in the forest."

"Has he, now?"

"Yes. My cousin, Jim, was working for him."

"Who else?" Ned asked.

"Jim worked for me, too. He kept my books."

Ned snorted as if he thought she was the most dull-witted person on the planet. "I mean, who else was working with Buford and Jimmy?"

"How should I know?" Trudy Lynn was getting aggravated. "You'd better shut off that light before Buford sees it."

"He's not going to see anything. Not from where he is."

She brightened. "The noise in the hall? Was that you? Did you knock him out?"

"Something like that."

"Praise God. My prayers were answered!"

"Still on your soapbox, I see," Ned remarked. "That's probably for the best. At least you think you'll go to heaven. That must be some comfort at a time like this."

Trudy Lynn instinctively started to inch away. Her ankle protested. "What are you talking about?"

"You couldn't leave well enough alone, could you? Had to go nosing into other people's business like you had a right. I've always hated that about you." He snorted. "Among other things."

"Then why did you ask me to marry you?"

"Haven't you figured that out by now? If you'd come to the city like you were supposed to, we wouldn't be having this discussion." He laughed menacingly. "You actually might have enjoyed being my wife for a while, at least until I got tired of you."

"You said you loved me!"

"I was good, wasn't I? Nobody suspected a thing. Not even your friends. Most of them were even on my side, trying to convince you to let go of this dump and move away. You should have listened to them. Why didn't you?"

Anger replaced astonishment, giving her courage. "Because I knew something was wrong between us. In my heart, I knew."

"Women's intuition?"

She shook her head. "No. God must have been warning me all along. I'm just thankful I listened."

"Really?" Ned perched on the corner of the mattress, his feet mere inches from where she lay on the floor. "Did He also tell you why I wanted you to leave here?"

"No, of course not." Her thoughts spun. Her eyes widened. It was all starting to tie together and make sense—the vandalism, the other camps closing, the location of the illegal crop and the greenhouse…Ned's insistence that she had to leave Serenity for his sake.

Squinting, she could see only a shadowy form behind the light but she could tell when his head nodded.

"I see you've figured it out." He got to his feet and towered over her. "Too bad. I was hoping our friend Buford would take care of this for me." He gave a sardonic chuckle. "Oh, well, at least he's not alive to deny it. That'll do."

"You *killed* him?"

"In self-defense," Ned drawled. "Too bad I got here too late to prevent him from killing you, first."

SEVENTEEN

Cody saw the beam of a flashlight moving through the lodge. Instead of burglar-like wandering, the light headed straight for Trudy Lynn's living quarters!

Rounding the corner of the store, Cody noticed a black sedan, parked where it couldn't be seen from the road. It was new. Clean. Expensive. If Buford had arrived in that, he'd sure come up in the world.

"Probably stole it," he muttered. Sailor loped up beside him, out of breath, tongue lolling. With his fur puffed out by aggression he looked even bigger than usual.

Cody grabbed the dog's collar. "Easy now. We'll do this together." He didn't want to endanger his best buddy but he figured Buford would be far more likely to back down if he saw he had a growling animal the size of a black bear to contend with.

The rear door stood ajar. Cody eased it open farther. Flashes of lightning glinted off shards of broken glass on the tile floor. He led Sailor around them to protect the dog's feet.

Muffled voices were drifting up the hall. The Newf

heard them, too. It leaped ahead, almost jerked loose, and headed down the dark passageway at a gallop, dragging Cody along like a water skier following the wake of a speedboat.

A sharp turn at the doorway scraped him off. Sailor never slowed. He crossed the room and hit the person holding the flashlight at full gallop.

Trudy Lynn screamed. Instinct told her to throw herself backward and cover her face with her arms.

Widget scrambled away, bounced off the wall and dashed into the fray, yipping wildly.

Above and to one side, a terrible fight was taking place. Men were shouting. Animals were growling and snapping. Fabric tore. Furniture crashed into the walls. Glass shattered.

Trudy Lynn managed to slide her injured ankle far enough under the bed to protect it. The rest of her was hunkered down as close to the box spring as possible.

Something soggy and hairy bumped into her. That odor! Wet dog! It had to be Sailor. Nothing else was that big or smelled quite that doggy when it was damp. And if Sailor was here, Cody must be!

A man grunted. A punch connected. A body hit the wall and slid to the floor beyond the dresser. Trudy Lynn held her breath and prayed that Cody was the one still on his feet.

Sailor's wagging tail began to slap her with a welcome cadence. He was no longer in attack mode! Someone was reaching for the discarded flashlight, picking it up. The beam once again swung in her direction.

"Cody?" she asked hopefully.

"I'm here," he answered. "Are you okay?"

"I am now."

"Thank God." It was definitely a prayerful statement.

"I'll second that," she said. "How did you know I was in trouble?"

"Sailor told me." Cody lowered himself to the edge of the bed and shined the flashlight on the crumpled attacker. "Whew! That was close. I thought…" The beam played over the man. "Hold it. That's not Buford."

"No," Trudy Lynn said sadly. "That's Ned."

"What's *he* doing here."

She shivered, suddenly chilled to the bone. "He just told me he killed Buford. He said he was going to kill me next and blame it on poor Buford."

Cody swung the light back to her face. "What?! Are you sure?"

"I'm afraid I am." Her lower lip began to quiver in spite of the immense relief of having Cody there. He offered his hand to her. She shook her head. "Sorry. I'd better sit tight till the paramedics arrive."

Cody leaned down beside her. "You said you were fine. What's wrong?"

"I think my ankle's broken."

"Show me."

"Uh-uh. It's safe under the bed. I had to crawl to get this far. I'm not moving one more inch on my own."

She saw him shine the light around the room, then return it to Ned. The other man was beginning to stir.

"Got any rope in here?" Cody asked.

"Will scarves do?"

"Belts would be better."

"In the closet. Hanging on a rack on the far right," Trudy Lynn said.

He returned and handed her the flashlight. "Hold this for me while I tie him up."

"Okay." The throbbing in her foot was beginning to keep her from thinking clearly. "I, um, I did call the police," she said. "I'm not sure they got the right information, though. Maybe you should call again."

"I already had Becky do that." Cody straightened. "The one thing I'm not sure of is whether or not Ned was alone."

"I did hear at least two sets of footsteps. I think one of them was Buford, though, before Ned took care of him." Her trembling had intensified so badly she couldn't hold the light steady.

"You're going into shock," Cody said flatly. "I won't take the chance of getting trapped in here with another lunatic. Two's my limit." He again held out his hand. "Come on. Either you help or I'll have to carry you."

Pain colored her answer, turned it harsh. "Oh, yeah? How? You can hardly walk, yourself."

"I'll manage. Well, what'll it be?"

"I'll help, I'll help," she said quickly. "Let me do it slowly. It really hurts."

"I believe that. Where are those scarves you said you had?"

"In the dresser. Bottom drawer. Why?"

"I'm going to make a splint to keep you from damaging that ankle any worse." He paused. "Is that okay or are you planning to argue?"

"Not me," Trudy Lynn managed brief movements punctuated with gasps and gritted teeth. "Where's Widget?"

"Standing on Ned's chest, snarling at him."

"Good. Anybody who calls my darling little dog a rat deserves to be treated like the rotten person he is." She winced. "I hope he rots in jail for everything he's done. I can't believe I ever considered marrying that scumbag."

"Neither can I." Cody returned with two plastic hangers and bent down. "Can you hold one of these on each side of your ankle while I wrap it? I'll be as gentle as possible."

"I know you will." His hands were tender, his movements patient. She'd made up her mind not to cry out and she succeeded except for one little mew.

"Sorry," Cody said.

"It's okay. I'm a wimp."

"If you are, you're the bravest one I've ever known," he countered. "There. I'm done. Ready to get up?"

"As ready as I'll ever be. Are you sure this is necessary?"

"Not positive, no. But I think it's wise."

She let him hoist her into a standing position, gritting her teeth to keep from crying out. "That's good enough for me," she said. "I trust your judgment."

"You *do*?"

His incredulity was almost enough to make her laugh in spite of her suffering. "Yes, I do. Come on. Let's get out of here before I change my mind."

"Your ankle's broken," Cody told Trudy Lynn later.

"Surprise, surprise." She winced. "What about Ned? Did the sheriff arrest him? Was he alone?"

"Yes, and yes. Jimmy identified the other men involved in the operation and they've already been picked up. The Drug Task Force is raiding the greenhouse as we speak. It's all over."

"Thank God for that," she whispered prayerfully.

"Sounds like you can thank Him for a monetary reward, too. The DEA chief told me your share should provide enough money to pay your staff retroactive wages after all."

"Unbelievable!"

Trudy Lynn had been given an injection to help her temporarily cope with the pain and she was starting to feel its effects. She smiled and sighed.

Cody took her hand. "Are you feeling any better?"

"Some. I think my ankle's throbbing less. Now, I'm freezing."

"That's because they've put ice on your leg," he explained. "Shall I ask a nurse to bring you another blanket?"

"No. Don't leave. Stay and talk to me? Please?"

"Sure. I've been wanting to have a talk with you anyway."

"Really?" Trudy Lynn's ears were buzzing and her

head felt funny, as if she were floating on a pillow of air instead of lying on a gurney in a hospital emergency room. "Me, too. Talk to you, I mean, not to myself."

"I figured as much." There was humor in his voice. "Maybe we'd better wait. You sound pretty out of it right now."

"Nonsense. I'm fine." She made a face. "I wasn't stupid. I know it must seem that way to you but I really wasn't. I mean, all my friends kept insisting Ned was the right man for me but I never bought it. He was too nice. Too perfect. Too…" She rolled her eyes. "I can't think of the right word. My brain's getting all fuzzy. Manipulative! That's it. Ned was always trying to get me to do things his way, only he was so sweet about it he made me sick."

"Trudy Lynn…"

"I should have known. I guess I did know. Like I told him when he was threatening to kill me, I think God was warning me all along. Does that make sense to you?"

"Yes." Cody stroked his thumb over the back of her hand as he held it and smiled at her. "I've been thinking…"

"Yeah, me, too. I didn't see it at first because I was too set in my ways, I guess. It wasn't that I wanted someone who never disagreed with me. I know I'm not perfect." She giggled. "Even if I am close to it."

Cody laughed softly. "Now, *that* we agree on."

"Oh, good, because I don't care if you're not—perfect, I mean. Forget the limp. It doesn't matter."

"I know that now."

"Hey! Maybe I'll limp, too!" She was grinning so

widely her cheek muscles cramped. "Wouldn't that be wonderful!"

"No, it wouldn't. I don't want anything to hurt you. Ever."

"Why not? Just think, we could have his and hers canes or something. I could tie a pink bow on mine so we could tell them apart!" That struck her so funny she burst into a fit of giggling.

"I'm afraid the medicine they gave you is making you loopy, honey."

"Who, me?" Trudy Lynn couldn't stop laughing, even when tears began to stream down her cheeks.

"Yes, you." Cody gave her a lopsided smile and shook his head. "You've been talking so much I haven't been able to get a word in."

"You did so. You said—something. I heard you."

He waited for her laughter to wane. "I've been trying to tell you I love you."

"Oh, sure, but…" She gasped. "You do?"

"Uh-huh. I'm crazy about you."

"Am I hallucinating?"

"I sure hope not because I'm asking you to marry me, too."

"That's it. I am hallucinating. I knew it." She made a quirky face at him, then blinked rapidly as if trying to clear her vision. "Who are you?"

"I'm Cody. Remember?"

"Nope. You can't be." Her voice was beginning to slur. Her eyelids drooped "You're being nice. Cody always argues with me."

"That's because you're so stubborn." He stood, bent and placed a kiss on her forehead. "Get some rest, honey. We'll talk more when you wake up."

Her fingers tightened on his. "Don't go," she mouthed almost soundlessly.

"I'll stay as long as you want me. How about fifty or sixty years?"

Trudy Lynn heard him speaking but couldn't rouse herself enough to answer. She'd long dreamed of what she'd say when the right man proposed marriage. Being rendered speechless by medication and hearing his profession of undying love while lying in a hospital awaiting treatment was *not* the romantic scenario she'd pictured.

Lost in joyful thoughts, she smiled. Cody Keringhoven wasn't the kind of man she'd envisioned, either. He was better. Much better. And as soon as she could make her voice work again she was going to tell him so.

Trudy Lynn awoke with a start, surprised to find she'd been moved to a hospital room. Then, the details came flooding back. She could have died. And now she was about to start really living.

Metal rails on her bed made perfect handholds. She pulled herself into a sitting position and looked around the portion of the room that wasn't curtained off for her roommate's privacy. Cody was slumped, snoring, in the only visible chair. His light-colored hair was tousled, his chin shadowed by a beard so blond it probably wouldn't have been noticeable in brighter light. He looked absolutely dear. And so exhausted she hated to wake him.

Apparently, her intense concentration was enough to break through. He yawned, stretched and began to smile the moment he saw her sitting up. "Hi. How are you feeling?"

"Wonderful."

"Your ankle doesn't hurt?"

"It's killing me." She grinned. "Say it again."

"Your ankle doesn't hurt?"

"No, silly. Way before that. Did you or didn't you ask me to marry you?"

"I might have." He grinned and reached for her hand.

"Well, if you didn't, I've just had the best dream of my entire life."

"What was your answer in this dream?"

"I said yes."

"That wasn't because you were groggy from the medication?"

"My thinking might have been hazy but yours wasn't. Did you say you loved me, or not?"

"I did. I'm glad it registered. You didn't seem real sure who I even was, let alone what I was trying to say."

"My heart knew," Trudy Lynn said. "I think it always knew everything, even when you were depressed and being so hard on yourself." She twisted so she could place her opposite hand atop his and watch his expression as she asked, "What about California?"

"Maybe we'll go there on our honeymoon before we settle down here, if that's all right with you."

Her heart was filled to bursting. "It sounds wonderful. I love you, Cody. All of you. Just as you are." She chuckled softly. "I even love your dog."

One eyebrow arched. "Uh-oh. Does that mean I have to fall madly in love with Widget, too?"

"I'm not that picky. As long as you honestly like him that's good enough for me."

"What a relief," Cody teased, "I was afraid you'd want him to be in the wedding party."

"No," she said, her eyes meeting his with a mischievous twinkle, "I thought we'd let Sailor carry the basket of flowers down the aisle."

"You're joking!"

Trudy Lynn giggled. "I was. Now that I think about it, that idea doesn't sound half-bad."

"Honey," Cody said, looking at her with so much love it made her heart and soul sing, "if that's what you want, it's okay with me."

"I think you mean that."

"I do. This time. Just don't get in the habit of expecting me to do things your way every time."

"Perish the thought," Trudy Lynn quipped. "I wouldn't respect you if you changed too much. However, we do have other, more pressing decisions to make."

"The ring? Your dress? I know those things matter to women. I do want to have Logan perform the ceremony."

"Of course. And Becky will be my Matron of Honor. That wasn't what I was worried about."

"Then what? There's nothing you and I can't handle if we work it out together."

She pointed to the temporary cast on her swollen

ankle. "I don't know how long it's going to take me to heal and I don't want to postpone our wedding for too long. Are you going to push me down the aisle in a wheelchair or shall we wait till I'm well enough to hobble?"

On the other side of the curtain between the beds, an elderly female patient tittered, then called, "Push her, son, push her. It'll probably be your last chance to be in charge for a good long time!"

EPILOGUE

Becky had decorated Trudy Lynn's wheelchair with enough flowers and pastel ribbons to keep it from looking utilitarian and was preparing to escort her down the aisle of Serenity Chapel.

"I told you I could walk," Trudy Lynn whispered.

"I know you did. And I'm sure you'd manage. Except the doctor wants you to keep your weight off that leg for another four weeks."

"Maybe we should have put things off longer, made it a double wedding with Will and Earlene, now that he's finally gotten around to officially asking her to marry him."

Becky leaned over the bride's shoulder to whisper, "Not if you expected me to fit into this dress."

"I know." Trudy Lynn suppressed a giggle. "Have you told anybody else?"

"Besides you and Logan and Cody, no," Becky said. "The rumors will start to fly soon enough. I imagine it'll be like the whole church is expecting this baby."

"And I'll be an aunt!"

"Not till you marry my brother. He's waiting for you."

Trudy Lynn beamed. She'd never seen her beloved Cody look so handsome, so appealing. What a blessing to know that they shared not only their love, but also their faith. Suddenly, all she wanted was to go to him. To be near him.

She spoke aside to Becky. "I'm ready. Let's roll."

"You're supposed to wait for the organist to start playing 'The Wedding March.'"

"And if I don't? I'll still be married, won't I?"

"Of course, but…"

Trudy Lynn was laughing lightly at the astonishment on her friend's face as she laid her bouquet in her lap and reached for the large side wheels on her beribboned chrome chariot. One strong push forward sent the chair over the edge of the flat section of floor in the rear of the sanctuary and onto the sloping aisle that led to the altar. To Cody. To her future. As the old saying went, it was "downhill all the way."

Cody elbowed Logan. "Looks like my bride is in a hurry. Either that or she's out of control."

"Knowing Trudy Lynn she's probably both," the pastor said with admiration. "Brace yourself. Here she comes."

Cody was laughing as he helped his future wife come to a full stop at the foot of the aisle. "Is that your last trick of the day or should I be ready for more?"

"I think I'm done." She was blushing. "I really didn't mean to go that fast."

"I know." Sobering, he lifted and supported her so she could stand beside him for the ceremony. "Don't worry. Whatever you do, I'll always be there to catch you," he promised quietly.

Trudy Lynn gazed at him through tears of thankfulness and incredible joy. "I wouldn't have it any other way."

* * * * *

Dear Reader,

In looking at the Scripture I chose for this book's theme, I was struck by how hard it sometimes is to accept the trials life brings us, whether they are only physical or go deeper as well, like Cody's did.

I don't pretend to have all the answers. Only in the realm of fiction can I make things work out the way I think they should. No one except God has the divine insight necessary to look ahead and see what the future holds for each of us, which is why I've decided to place my life in His hands, no matter what. Yes, I still slip and argue that my way is best from time to time, but in my heart I know that the Lord is patiently, lovingly watching over me—in the best and the worst of times.

If you don't have the assurance that you're God's child, I urge you to seek it. All you have to do is surrender your pride, ask Jesus to forgive and accept you right now, and He will. It's that easy.

I love to hear from readers. The quickest replies are by e-mail—valw@centurytel.net—or you can write me at P.O. Box 13, Glencoe, AR 72539, and I'll do my best to answer as soon as I can spare time away from my latest manuscript. My Web site is www.valeriehansen.com.

Blessings,

Valerie Hansen

QUESTIONS FOR DISCUSSION

1. Cody was upset to have to ask for help from his family. Has this ever happened to you? Did you delay asking rather than admit a need?

2. If you did ask for help, how did you feel afterward? Were you glad you had admitted you needed help?

3. Looking back, can you see the Lord's hand in the situation? How?

4. If you were the one giving the assistance instead of the one taking it, were you blessed to have been able to help?

5. Have you ever prayed for something the way Cody did, then given up on God when you didn't get the answer you thought you should?

6. Cody had made his previous career the focus of his whole life. Trudy still does. Have you ever known someone who was so caught up in a job or hobby that they became obsessed by it? Was that a good thing? Did it bring them lasting happiness or were they still missing something to fulfill their lives?

7. Trudy finds solace and peace in the place she lives. Would she have been as happy somewhere else if she kept her heart and mind focused on God's will?

8. The villain who attacks Trudy in the woods is clearly a menace. Is it always that easy to spot evil? Why or why not?

9. Have you ever felt that others have advantages that you don't, such as skills or talents or even more money? Is that what makes a person valuable to God?

10. Trudy prays for Cody's healing. If he isn't totally healed, will that mean God has not answered her prayer? Can you see that the answer may be different than she expected, yet better for everyone?

REQUEST YOUR FREE BOOKS!

2 FREE INSPIRATIONAL NOVELS
PLUS 2
FREE
MYSTERY GIFTS

YES! Please send me 2 FREE Love Inspired® novels and my 2 FREE mystery gifts. After receiving them, if I don't wish to receive any more books, I can return the shipping statement marked "cancel." If I don't cancel, I will receive 4 brand-new novels every month and be billed just $3.99 per book in the U.S., or $4.74 per book in Canada, plus 25¢ shipping and handling per book and applicable taxes, if any*. That's a savings of at least 20% off the cover price! I understand that accepting the 2 free books and gifts places me under no obligation to buy anything. I can always return a shipment and cancel at any time. Even if I never buy another book from Steeple Hill, the two free books and gifts are mine to keep forever.

113 IDN EF26 313 IDN EF27

Name	(PLEASE PRINT)	
Address		Apt.
City	State/Prov.	Zip/Postal Code

Signature (if under 18, a parent or guardian must sign)

Order online at www.LoveInspiredBooks.com

Or mail to Steeple Hill Reader Service™:

IN U.S.A.	**IN CANADA**
P.O. Box 1867	P.O. Box 609
Buffalo, NY	Fort Erie, Ontario
14240-1867	L2A 5X3

Not valid to current Love Inspired subscribers.

Want to try two free books from another series?
Call 1-800-873-8635 or visit www.morefreebooks.com

* Terms and prices subject to change without notice. NY residents add applicable sales tax. Canadian residents will be charged applicable provincial taxes and GST. This offer is limited to one order per household. All orders subject to approval. Credit or debit balances in a customer's account(s) may be offset by any other outstanding balance owed by or to the customer. Please allow 4 to 6 weeks for delivery.

LIREG06

Love Inspired SUSPENSE

TITLES AVAILABLE NEXT MONTH

Don't miss these two stories in January

HEART OF THE AMAZON by Margaret Daley

Kate Collier needed to search the Amazon to find her missing brother. To do that, she had to rely on guide A. C. Slader. Their journey would stretch the limit of their faith in God and each other, for it was a journey from which many never returned.

FATAL IMAGE by Lenora Worth
The Secrets of Stoneley

Bianca Blanchard never questioned her mother's death until Leo Santiago gave her a picture of their mothers—dated a week *after* her mother's death. Now Bianca won't rest until she finds out the truth, but are some secrets better left buried?

LISCNM1206